Super Powerful Organization Of Terriers and Songbird

S.P.O.T.S.

Franklin Young

AWESOME BOOKS

PROLOGUE

The name of the guy driving the delivery truck is not important. What does matter is the fact that he was driving like a maniac.

And that matters because a mile up ahead, an unmarked black Army truck was pulled over on the side of the highway. The truck had a flat tire and was being guarded by three commandoes who were completely dressed in black.

Back in the delivery truck, the driver noticed a blimp hovering over the highway. Having only seen blimps on TV, the sight of a real one caused him to stare in fascination.

He kept looking up when he should have been looking straight ahead. Somewhere deep inside the speed-crazed driver's brain, a thought was born. And that thought was a simple one - "Eyes on the road!"

The driver snapped his eyes down from the blimp and back towards the highway, but it was too late.

He slammed his foot down on the brakes, and all eighteen wheels locked. There was a horrible screech and black smoke rose from his tires as he slammed into the back of the Army truck.

The force of the collision sent his cargo flying. Some of his shipment burst through the canvas side of the Army truck where it knocked over dozens of barrels that then spilled their orange, gooey load. The rest of the driver's shipment was spread out all over the highway where it was slowly being covered by the guck dripping out of the Army truck.

Until the situation on the highway could be cleaned up, thousands of people would be stranded in their cars, vans and trucks. All because the truck that the driver had slammed into was part of an important government operation: it had been hauling away radioactive waste from a secret research facility.

Soon, the Hazardous Materials (or "HazMat") team would arrive to clean up the mess. But, with a radioactive spill to clean, a busy highway to re-open and an Army's secret to protect, the HazMat team had a lot of work ahead of them. They'd be so busy over the next few hours that it's not surprising they didn't notice that a few of the boxes were missing.

And those boxes would soon change many lives in a nearby neighborhood.

HEROES AND VILLAINS

In the off-leash area of a park near the highway, five friends were sniffing each other. It's not as weird as it sounds, because these friends were all dogs. More specifically, they were Terriers, and they are the heroes of this story. The unofficial leader of the pack was Molly, an old and chunky Bull Terrier. Checking out her scent was Buck, a handsome Irish Terrier who had once been a performer in a traveling dog show.

While the two larger dogs snorted at each other, their smaller friends were also getting nasally reacquainted. Georgie the feisty West Highland Terrier (more simply known as a "Westie") was sniffing her grumpy pal Duffy. As a Dandie Dinmont Terrier, Duffy was one of the silliest looking dogs around. He compensated for the poofiness of his fur by walking around as if he was constantly looking for a fight. The smallest, youngest and bounciest member of the group was Jackie, a Jack Russell Terrier who was too excited to take more than a brief whiff of his friends. He wasn't excited about anything in particular; Jack Russells are just always keyed up.

While the Terriers were performing their daily ritual of greeting each other, a group of dog-haters were quietly gathering nearby. These cruel and thuggish creatures were the sworn enemies of all dogs, and they would do anything to destroy them.

For they were cats, and that's what cats do.

At the same time, dogs are also not big fans of cats. In fact, a recent survey of dogs showed that 99.9% of them would not be unhappy if a giant vacuum cleaner came down from outer space and sucked every last cat up and off of the face of the earth.

The Terriers often wondered why some humans chose to bring cats into the neighborhood. As far as they were concerned, cats are selfish, snobbish litter box dwellers. Worse, they aren't even fun to chase like squirrels. Because sometimes cats stop running, start hissing and begin to flail their claws. And those claws can hurt. Which is just one of many reasons why dogs can't stand being around cats.

Back in the park, Duffy was the first one to catch the scent.

"Stop the sniffing guys. We've got cats." It should be mentioned that Duffy very often stated the obvious. This way, he could claim that he was never wrong.

Molly, Buck, Georgie and Jackie turned to look at the cats who were slowly licking themselves as they stared back at the Terriers.

"There goes the neighborhood," sneered Georgie just loud enough for the cat gang to hear.

The leader of the cats - a nasty black and white named Peter - stopped licking his leg. He looked over at the dogs and let out a low hiss.

"It'th our park too." Then for good measure, he added, "you dumb dogth!" Peter then returned to cleaning himself.

Buck shook his head.

"Didn't your mama tell you not to speak with fur in your mouth?"

While the other Terriers barked happily at the insult, Peter turned to his huge, hairless and psychotic hench-cat Patches. With a slight jerk of his head, Peter sent him stalking towards the Terriers.

"You're pretty funny for a bunch of ball fetchers," snarled Patches.

"Thanks," said Georgie. "We ARE pretty funny, aren't we?"

Patches arched his back and hissed.

"I must have left my sense of humor at home. Because I ain't laughing!"

He then unsheathed his claws and put his paw in Georgie's face.

Georgie stopped smiling. Buck, who claimed to have never backed down from a fight, jumped towards Patches.

"Go ahead Baldy,"' he said in a calm, steady voice. "Just try it."

"Don't challenge him!" Georgie growled at Buck. "It's my eyes he's going to scratch out!"

Molly shook her head as she stepped towards Patches.

"The only things he's going to scratch are his Mama's curtains. Isn't that right Patches?"

Patches could sense the rest of the cats behind him. Peter, Puss Puss, Petunia and Precious hissed in unison as they joined the fray. The five cats struck a pose with their claws extended. They clearly meant business, except for Precious who looked like she was auditioning for a part in a cat food commercial.

Molly looked at her friends who were hunched down with their rear ends in the air. Their teeth were bared and they too were ready for action. She then glanced from the Terriers to the cats. All of them were ready to rumble.

"I want the dumb one!" snarled Puss Puss who was actually pretty bright… for a cat.

"Which one?" asked Precious who then paused for comedic effect. "They're dogs, so they're all dumb."

The sound of five cats laughing filled the air.

"What, what, WHAT are we waiting for?!" barked Jackie.

"We're waiting for them to cross the line," said Molly.

"Ummm, which line?" asked Petunia.

As far as any of them could see, there wasn't a line on the ground.

Peter rolled his eyes. "It'th a metaphor you idiot! He meanth if we take one more thtep, the fight ith on!"

Petunia was about to ask what a "metaphor" is, but he never got the chance. It was at that precise moment that the two snarling and hissing groups of pets heard the "BANG!" of the jerky truck colliding with the secret government trailer.

DOGS PIG OUT

As the sound of the collision echoed through the park, the cats did what cats normally do in a noisy situation and ran home to hide under their couches.

"They're running away," shouted Duffy, once again saying what everyone already knew.

"What a bunch of SCAREDY-CATS!" joked Georgie.

"What, what WHAT was that noise?" shouted Jackie.

"Dunno," said Buck. "Sounded kind of ominous like."

Not knowing what the word "ominous" meant, the other dogs turned to Molly for an explanation. She may have been the wisest of the Terriers, but at the moment, she was too busy sniffing the air to be able to explain anything.

"It smells like snacks," she said.

The five Terriers inhaled at the same time. No doubt about it, the park did suddenly have the fine aroma of juicy snacks. And when the promise of tasty food is in the air, it is very hard for a dog to keep still. So even though they may have been "ominous" snacks, the Terriers took off.

They hadn't gone far when Molly barked for them to stop. Up above on the overpass, traffic was backed up for miles as angry drivers honked at the soldiers who had shut down the highway.

But Molly could barely hear the noise. She was busy sniffing one of the greatest scents she had ever smelled.

"Follow me!" she howled as she ran into the bushes.

Buck, Jackie, Duffy and Georgie chased after her. When they got to the bushes, their eyes and mouths popped open as they saw some of the Driver's spilled cargo. It was a dog's dream come true as there, right in front of them, were several boxes of meat jerky snacks.

There were smashed open cartons of beef jerky, bacon jerky, chicken jerky and even, yes, turkey jerky. That's right, there's actually a product called "turkey jerky." Say it four times fast, and you'll see exactly how silly it sounds.

The five Terriers stalked towards the broken boxes of jerky. They had trouble believing their noses and eyes - a small mountain of unguarded meat strips seemed too good to be true. The Terriers were so excited that they didn't notice that most of the jerky pieces were coated in glowing orange goo.

"Must be some kind of dream." Whispered Buck.

"Dreams don't taste like this!" said Molly as she picked up a piece of bacon jerky.

Even though she lacked a couple of teeth, it only took two bites for her to introduce the jerky to her stomach.

"Oh! Oh that's good," she said as she picked up another piece. "What are you guys waiting for?"

"Snack. Snack! SNACK TIME!!!" yipped Jackie as he and the others attacked the jerky.

It was a Terrier feeding frenzy. Jaws clenched, boxes were shredded and mouths and stomachs were filled with every dog's dream meal. In a few short minutes, all the jerky had been devoured, and the five Terriers were stuffed full of salty snack meats.

They didn't know it, but they were also full of radioactive waste that was going to change them forever. Molly, Georgie, Buck and Duffy collapsed on the ground, happily clutching at their distended bellies.

"That was more than just good," moaned Duffy happily. "That was the best thing ever."

Georgie tried to respond, but when she opened her mouth, all that came out was a St. Bernard-sized belch. She smiled happily as she rolled onto her back.

"Hey! I found more! More!! MORE!!!" Jackie yelled.

The Terriers slowly got to their feet and waddled over to where Jackie was sniffing at another broken box of jerky.

This batch didn't have the salty, meaty smell that drives dogs crazy. Instead, it smelled gross and dirty. Kind of like garbage, but not the kind of garbage that dogs like. No, this carton stunk like old fish. Which made sense, because it was full of cod jerky. Even without a coating of radioactive guck, no dog or human would eat such a disgusting snack.

The Terriers took a deep sniff of the uneaten jerky. Georgie gagged and almost barfed.

"It really stinks."

Just to be sure, she took one more deep sniff.

Buck shook his head and stepped away from the foul-smelling cod jerky.

"Nothing I'm going to eat," he said as he started to walk away.

"We'd better get back to the humans," said Molly. "You know we can't leave them on their own for too long."

As the Terriers staggered away from the bushes, they looked back at the scene of their feast. This was the kind of wonderful occasion that was made even better by being shared with the best friends that any dog could ever have. They knew that something this special might never happen again.

"Good times," said Georgie wistfully. "Good times indeed."

Then she burped.

BAD GAS AND WEIRD DREAMS

That night was a tough one for the Terriers. Even though their bellies were stuffed with jerky, when dinner was served, they still managed to eat all of the dog food and table scraps that they were offered.

They may not have been hungry, but they were dogs.

However, the overeating made it hard for them to get comfortable in their beds. They tossed, they turned and then they released gas that was created by feasting on bad snack foods. Which means that the Terriers' families also had rough nights.

Amidst the jerky fumes, the Terriers did manage to fall asleep. And when they did, boy oh boy, were their dreams ever strange.

GEORGIE VERSUS THE MAILMAN

The first Terrier to fall asleep was Georgie who always slept in the big bed with her human Mrs. G.. Some would say that the fact they shared a king-sized bed was a case of someone being spoiled. But Georgie figured that since Mrs. G. didn't take up too much space, it wasn't such a big deal to let her stay in the bed with her.

In her dream, Georgie was standing in the darkened living room watching as a large, menacing shadow crept closer to the house. Georgie's muscles tensed and her lips curled. With her teeth bared, she was ready for whatever danger was approaching. Then darkness flooded the room as she got a glimpse of the beast that was moving towards the front door.

Georgie had never seen anything so scary. It was huge... it was relentless... it was every dog's nightmare; a giant Mailman who carried a massive stack of mail and magazines.

BAM!!

The front steps of the house were ground into dust as the Mailman's huge boot crushed down. His massive gloved hand slowly moved forward and tried to jam the letters and magazines through the mail slot in the front door.

BUT THE STACK WAS TOO BIG! IT WOULDN'T FIT!

Georgie's eyes widened as she realized that the Mail-monster wouldn't stop. He kept stabbing the stack at the slot!

Then came a WHAM! as the mail slot shattered and the door started to crack. WHAM! WHAM! WHAM! The stack of mail was breaking the door into splinters.

Georgie watched in horror, knowing that if the door fell, the giant Mailman would be able to come in the house and steal her food. Not just the bowl of kibble on the floor either. He'd be able to empty the cupboards and the fridge. Talk about a nightmare! A house without food?! No way was that going to happen on her watch!

Georgie stepped forward and let out a series of barks that started loudly and quickly reached ear-shattering levels.

"RWOWF!!!"

"RWOWF!!!"

"RWOWF!!!"

"RWOWF!!!"

The Mailman tried to cover his ears, but he was too slow. The vibrations from the barks caused his head to explode.

Literally.

With his head gone, it didn't take long for the Mailman's body to collapse into a pile of chunks and crumbs that looked like a huge pile of crushed dog biscuits. Just to make sure that he was well and truly vanquished, Georgie walked out of the house and ate the cookie-flavored pieces of the Mailman. She then barked in triumph. For not only had she defeated a Mail-monster; she had eaten him as well.

It was Georgie's flailing that finally woke Mrs. G.. Since she never wore her hearing aid to bed, she had no way of knowing just how incredibly loud Georgie's barks had been. But the shattered window let her know that something strange had happened in the bedroom.

Mrs. G. looked from the broken window over to Georgie who was now half-awake and trying in vain to taste the Mailman.

"What happened here Girl?" she asked.

If you can imagine a dog shrugging, then you can visualize what Georgie did in response to the question. She was just as confused as Mrs. G..

MOLLY THE HOME WRECKER

Meanwhile down the street, Molly was also having a wild dream. This wasn't surprising considering the amount of spiced jerky that was making its way through her digestive system. You see, when the body is trying to push out bad food, it somehow causes the brain to create nightmares. There's a scientific reason for this, but the explanation involves a lot of long confusing words and basically means that Hungarian salami is not a good late night snack.

In Molly's dream, a fresh tennis ball bounced along the sidewalk. She ran after the ball as fast as her bowed legs could carry her, but just couldn't quite get her teeth on it. Suddenly, the ball changed directions and bounced through an open doorway and into a big old mansion. Molly ran to the house, but just before she got inside, the huge door slammed shut. Molly didn't slow down and ran right through the door.

She stopped to look at the pieces of the door that lay all around her. None of the wood shards looked chewable, so Molly continued her search for the ball. She couldn't see it, but she could feel the vibrations as it kept on bouncing in a room behind the nearby concrete wall.

If she was awake, Molly would have looked for a door or another opening so she could walk into the room. But this was a dream... a dream where Molly felt stronger than she had ever felt in her life. She felt as powerful as ten, twelve, even fifteen Bull Terriers as she turned and backed towards the wall.

The thumping vibrations of the bouncing ball became stronger. Molly stayed calm, lifted her back legs and gave a mighty kick.

DOUBLE BAM! as the wall collapsed. Bricks rained down around her - in slow motion for an even more dramatic effect - as Molly calmly stepped forward and caught the bouncing tennis ball in her mouth.

"BLECCH!"

The ball tasted like bricks and cement which are things that most humans (and most dogs for that matter) have never tasted. Most likely though, it's a pretty awful flavor.

Molly spat out the ball which flew from her mouth with the approximate velocity of a bazooka shell. The ball shot through the front wall of the house, causing it to collapse completely.

As Molly walked away from the wrecked house, she didn't look back at the destruction. She was too busy searching for another tennis ball.

No doubt about it, she was young again, and she felt so powerful that she was able to do whatever she wanted. On a scale of one to ten, she'd have to give this dream a perfect ten.

Which equals a perfect seventy on the human dream scale.

BUCK TO THE RESCUE

A few houses away, Buck was sleeping in his reclining chair. In spite of his rumbling stomach, it was a deep and very happy sleep.

Some people claim that dogs don't smile. Their tails can wag, and their eyes can light up with excitement, but they believe that dogs can't smile like humans. Of course, the people who say this haven't had a dog in their family. Or if they have, they didn't do enough to actually make the dog smile.

Buck's family did a lot to make him smile, and he was a very happy, healthy dog. At this point however, it was his dream that was making Buck grin...

The dream had begun in a large theater where a smoke machine poured out some very dramatic fog. Buck walked onto the stage and bowed to the applauding humans and panting dogs in the audience. He was in mid-bow when a mixture of screams and barks snapped him to his senses.

"Buck! Help me!" It was the pretty collie that Buck used to sniff during his days as a performer in the "Phenomenal Dogs" show. She was being stolen by a tall man in dark clothes.

What was her name again? Buck couldn't think of it and it was driving him crazy. He really liked her, and she'd probably be upset if he didn't remember her name.

"Think!" he thought.

He knew it started with a "B," but he couldn't figure out if it was "Bella," "Barbie" or something more exotic, like...

"I've got Bebeto," yelled the tall man in dark clothes.

Of course! "Bebeto." How could he have forgotten?

Buck thought about how Bebeto was really a pretty name. He also thought about how amazing Bebeto smelled, and how her long fur was always so beautifully brushed.

"Come on already! He's stealing me!" barked Bebeto. "Stop thinking about my fur and help me! NOW!"

Buck snapped to attention, and realized that the theater was laid out for a "Phenomenal Dogs" show. All the obstacles and jumps were set up just like he remembered from his days in the show.

He looked out at the audience and snarled dramatically. As the crowd cheered and barked its encouragement, Buck ran after Bebeto and the dognapper. For some strange reason, the Bad Guy ran through the slalom cones. That was a big mistake. You see, during his days in the show, Buck was called "The Canine King of the Cones."

With each zig to the right and zag to the left of a cone, Buck got closer to Bebeto. He could see Bebeto's pretty tail flapping against the villain's coat.

"What a nice tail," he thought.

"Never mind my tail! Just stop this guy!" Bebeto barked.

After chasing the man away from the cones and up and down the giant teeter-totters, Buck was getting tired. As he fought to catch his breath, the Bad Guy ran out the theater door with Bebeto in his arms. The door slammed shut and automatically locked from the outside.

For the first time, Buck doubted himself. It looked like there was no way he could rescue the Doggess Bebeto.

He was about to give up hope when the audience of humans and dogs started to chant and bark his name.

"Buck!"

"Rowf!"

"Buck!"

"Rowf!"

Buck smiled and nodded at his fans. He then saw the trampoline near the stage and smirked. Bouncing on it was his favorite part of the "Phenomenal Dogs" show.

"I'm coming Bebeto!" he barked as he began his run. At just the right moment, Buck jumped and soared towards the trampoline.

Buck sproinged off the stretched canvas on the trampoline and soared up, up, up, waaay up. Just before he hit the ceiling of the theater, he tilted to his right, ducked his head and flew out of an open window. As Buck sailed towards the parking lot, he saw the Bad Guy carrying away the dog of his dreams.

Buck gritted his teeth, stuck out his paws and went into a dive. He landed in front of the man and let out his fiercest growl.

"Ha!" laughed the man. "You're pretty scary... for an Irish Setter."

In his sleep, Buck's blood began to heat up. His muscles tensed and his lips curled. Strangest of all was that his stomach began to churn and bubble.

The Bad Guy stepped back, a look of fear on his face.

As Buck got ready to speak, a strange taste filled his mouth. He didn't have time to worry about it, as he had just thought of the perfect response.

"Don't ever call me a 'Setter.' I am a 'TERRIER!'"

As the word "Terrier" echoed through the night, a greenish belch of mist shot out of Buck's mouth. The mist floated towards the Bad Guy who took one breath and immediately passed out. As he fell, Bebeto jumped out of his arms and stepped towards her rescuer.

Bebeto whispered in a soft and kind of romantic way, "you're my hero."

She then nuzzled up close to Buck who tried to look cool as his tail wagged at a truly incredible speed. He'd defeated the bad guy, won the paw of a cute girl and received a huge round of applause and happy barks from the audience. What more could a dog ask from a dream?

And as Buck dreamed on, you'd have marveled that a medium-sized dog could have such a big smile on its face.

DUFFY'S BIG STEAK

Around the corner from Buck, Duffy was snoring away in the kids' playhouse in the basement.

When they first brought Duffy into their lives, his family didn't want him to sleep in the expensive playhouse. They blocked its entrance with a baby gate, but Duffy easily squirmed under it. They then tried to distract him with an officially licensed, hypoallergenic dog bed that came complete with a pillow in the shape of "Boopy! Everyone's favorite cartoon dog!"

Duffy didn't like it, so he tore Boopy to pieces and then ripped apart the bed.

As a last resort, his adult humans decided to let Duffy sleep with them. They figured this would keep Duffy out of the kids' playhouse. After all, didn't every dog like to sleep on a human bed?

In truth, most dogs <u>love</u> sleeping with their humans. But no matter how many times his humans picked him up and put him on their bed, he would jump right back down. You see, Duffy DID like the big bed. But he also liked sleeping in the playhouse. And until his family was fully trained, he couldn't let them get what they wanted.

For you see, this is the way of the Terrier.

On this particular evening, as Duffy slept in HIS playhouse, he dreamt of a smell. Not just any aroma, for this was the mouthwatering, knee-weakening scent of a medium-rare rib steak.

In the dream, Duffy followed the steak smell into a darkened house that he had never seen before. As his eyes adjusted to the gloom, he saw the steak. And it was a beauty. At least sixteen ounces of beefy perfection. But there was a problem. A BIG problem. The steak was dangling from the mouth of a huge wall of muscle, teeth, jawbone and bad intentions.

It was in the mouth of a Pit Bull.

Unlike most dogs and most smart people, Duffy wasn't afraid of Pit Bulls. In fact, he was basically fearless and lived his life by the motto "I'm Not Ascared of Nothing!" Some would say that a dog as small as Duffy really shouldn't be so stubbornly brave, but he felt that he didn't have a choice. If he showed any fear at all, the bigger dogs in the neighborhood would take advantage of him. That could be dangerous for a small Dandie Dinmont.

So Duffy growled at the Pit Bull who dropped the steak, yelped in fear and ran away with its tail between its legs. Of course, in real life, the Pit Bull would have probably stuffed Duffy into its mouth next to the steak. But this wasn't real life. It was Duffy's dream.

Before Duffy could sink his teeth into the steak, it grew a pair of wings and flew down a darkened hallway. Duffy chased the flying steak but as he came to the end of the hall, all he could see were three doors, each one lit by a single spotlight. Duffy knew that the steak was behind a door and that he could only choose to open one of them. He also knew that he had only a single chance to find the meat, so he did what any dog would do; he took a deep sniff. But he just couldn't pick up the scent of the steak.

That's when something really weird happened. Maybe not as weird as a Dandy Dinmont scaring a Pit Bull, but pretty strange anyway. As Duffy looked up, he found that he could see through the doors! He had X-ray vision!

Behind the first door, Duffy saw something horrifying. Standing inside the small room was a nasty Groomer holding up a pair of clippers that reflected a scary-looking red light.

Pure evil.

Duffy stepped away from the Groomer's room and looked through the next door. This vision was even more awful than the first one. It was his Veterinarian, and she was pointing a large thermometer and an even larger needle right at him.

Purer evil.

Duffy let out a frightened "YIP" and jumped to the final door. As he looked through the door, he saw the steak sitting on a plate next to a huge bowl of cold water. Duffy smiled as he nudged the door open and stepped into the best part of the best dream he'd ever had.

That night throughout Duffy's home, there echoed a sound that none of the humans had ever heard before. It was the sound of a dog happily chewing in his sleep.

JACKIE & THE EXPLODING RODENTS

In a nearby house, Jackie was sitting up in his bed wondering if he should go to sleep. Jackie had a condition that made him unable to shut his eyes until the house was absolutely silent. There's a long and complicated word that veterinarians use to describe this condition. That word is "BeingaJackrussellterrier-itis."

And poor Jackie had a bad case of BeingaJackrussellterrier-itis. But once the kids were asleep, and once the adults had turned off the TV, and once the swing set stopped creaking and once the dishwasher stopped running... then, and only then, did Jackie allow his eyes to close.

Soon after he fell asleep, he began to dream. The first thing he saw in his dream were the three older kids - Sadie, Mitch and Joel - running out of the house. They were closely followed by Jordana in her suddenly self-propelled stroller. Jackie ran after them, but it was clearly just a dream; because unlike in real life, he couldn't catch up. He wasn't worried, just upset that he couldn't run next to them like he always did. After a short while, the kids arrived at their school. The three kids on legs ran into the school, while Jordana's stroller simply rolled in.

Jackie stopped near the school's front door because he knew that he shouldn't go inside. After all, every time that he tried, his full grown woman Nancy would yell and tell him that he was a "bad dog." But Nancy wasn't around. Neither was his full grown man Mike or anyone else. Jackie didn't want to be a "bad dog," but the door of the school WAS wide open.

He was tormented until he heard what sounded like a chipmunk in the school. At a time like that, you can tell a Terrier that it's "bad," but it won't make any difference. There's just <u>no</u> way a Terrier stands still when there's a rodent around.

Jackie sprinted into the school. At first, he couldn't see any chipmunks, and he didn't know which way to go. The school seemed to be nothing but hallways leading to other hallways, all of which were empty.

"Jackie boy!" Sadie's voice echoed through the school.

When Sadie called, Jackie always came running. He took off and turned the first corner, and that's when he saw something so shocking, it made him hit the brakes. This looked pretty funny, because the floor had just been polished and Jackie slid across the floor past a bunch of classrooms. When he finally stopped sliding, Jackie was inches from hundreds and hundreds of rodents.

Chipmunks, mice, lemmings, ferrets, jerboas, weasels, rats and even flying squirrels were lined up as far as his eyes could see.

Strangely, none of the rodents were trying to run away from Jackie. Rodents may have brains that are the size of jelly beans, but they usually have enough sense to run away when they see a Terrier. Even a dumb mouse knows that dogs like Jackie were originally bred to track them down and send them to vermin heaven.

Jackie was about to lunge at the rodents when he noticed that they didn't smell anything like the squirrels that ran through his yard. These ones stunk like the balloons that Nancy put all over the house for Mitch's birthday. Jackie remembered that Mitch's party was the last time he saw balloons in the house. That was because Jackie attacked every balloon he could find and bit them.

Chomping the balloons was fun, but it got Jackie in a lot of trouble with his humans. And Jackie couldn't stand it when he got in trouble. Just ten minutes into his dream and Jackie was already facing a second dilemma. Should he attack, or should he just sit still like a "good boy?"

Suddenly, a voice boomed out.

"Get 'em!" yelled Joel.

Jackie couldn't see Joel, but he didn't have to be told twice. With the decision made for him, he took a breath and pounced on a squirrel-shaped balloon.

BITE! POP!!!

Next was a mouse balloon.

BITE! POP!!!

Then it was time to take care of an inflated chipmunk.

BITE! POP!!!

For the next couple of hours, Jackie dreamt about biting his way through hallways filled with rodent balloons.

That night, all the Terriers enjoyed the best dreams that they had ever had. As they slept, they were no longer small dogs who were taken for granted and sometimes even laughed at by bigger dogs. In their dreams, they were stronger, smarter and more powerful than they had ever been.

And as the sun rose the next morning, their dreams were about to come true.

DISCOVERY AFTER DISCOVERY

On their way to the park the next day, the Terriers pulled extra hard on their leashes. Even Molly, who normally walked next to her big human Susan as she pushed the stroller that held her smaller human Emma, was way out in front. Molly was so excited to tell her friends about her crazy dream that she actually barked for Susan to "hurry up!"

When they finally got to the park and Molly was let off the leash, she ran as quickly as her old legs could take her. She bounced past the other Terriers' humans who were in their usual spot, chatting with each other and playing with Jordana who, like Emma, was too young for school.

When Molly reached her friends, she realized that her story was going to have to wait as Jackie was dramatically recreating his dream.

"BITE! POP!!! BITE! POP!!! BITE! POP!!! BITE! POP!!!" he yapped.

"We get the point already," said Duffy. "You broke a lot of balloons"

Jackie smiled at the memory.

"It was a great, great, GREAT dream. The best ever!"

"I also had a wonderful dream," Molly said.

"Join the club!" said Georgie. "We ALL did. I dreamed that my barks were so loud they made the mailman explode!"

As she remembered the dream, Georgie let out a happy bark that was so loud it caused the fence around the park to rattle and sway.

Georgie looked at her shocked friends.

"That was pretty loud wasn't it?" she asked unnecessarily.

"Even I heard it clearly" answered Molly.

Just then, the dogs - except Molly - heard footsteps. Four of them couldn't see who was coming, because a thick hedge blocked their view. Duffy however, saw the person clearly.

"It's Buck's Judy," he said, a second or two before she came into view.

"Hey guys!" Human Judy said. "We heard a loud bark. Is everything okay?"

People who don't have dogs sometimes wonder why humans speak to them and ask them questions. It's not as if they expect the dogs to answer them in their own language. It does seem kind of silly. But not as silly as when a human tries to speak dog.

Anyway, Judy saw that the five dogs were okay. They looked so cute that she was tempted to stick around and play with them. And she might have, if her cell phone hadn't gone off.

"Love to stay, but I have to take this call."

As Judy walked back to her human friends, Jackie had a revelation:

"I, I, I think I know what those beeping things are!" he said as he pointed at the cell phone.

"Those things pour food into the humans' ears."

"Are you crazy?" asked Georgie. "Humans eat through their mouths, just like us."

"Yeah?!" said Jackie. "Then why do they always, always, ALWAYS have those things stuck to their heads?"

As the Terriers thought about Jackie's strange theory, something occurred to Molly.

"How'd you know it was Judy before she got here?" she asked Duffy. "That hedge was between her and us."

"I just saw right through it." said Duffy. "It's weird... I could also see through things in my dream last night!"

"And I dreamed that my breath could make humans fall over," said Buck.

The Terriers were about to make a joke about Buck's bad breath when he stopped them by letting out a deep, horrible mouthful of mist.

The mist floated towards the soccer goalposts. The Terriers watched in awe as Buck's breath mist melted the posts before it dissipated into the wind.

"Something strange is going on here," said Duffy who, as mentioned earlier, had the very human talent of stating the obvious.

The dogs turned to face Molly who was the best of the bunch when it came to figuring things out. But Molly wasn't trying to solve the mystery of the Terriers' new powers. Instead, she was thinking about her own dream.

"I could run into walls and knock them down," she said. "Do you think I might be that powerful?"

"You could find out by running into the gardener's shed," suggested Buck.

Molly looked at the large brick shed and shook her head. If she really didn't have super strength, slamming into the shed's walls would definitely hurt.

She then noticed something half-hidden by giant weeds. Molly walked over to investigate, and the other Terriers followed. As they got close, they saw that it was a plaster statue of a cat.

"I've seen this, this, THIS thing before!" yipped Jackie. "It's a fake cat that's meant to look like that live cat that is now a dead cat!"

What Jackie meant was that the statue was a memorial that had been put up by someone to honor her cat who had passed away. It's kind of mean, but it made the dogs laugh.

"You know what they say," said Molly. "The only good cat..."

"Is a dead cat!" the others barked in unison.

As the Terriers giggled at their joke, Molly gritted her teeth and tensed her muscles.

"Goodbye Kitty," she growled as she ran towards the statue.

WHAM! Molly slammed into the statue and shattered its base. The plaster cat flew up and spun crazily as it cleared a fence and sailed towards a nearby backyard swimming pool. The Terriers watched as the statue splashed into the pool. It bobbed briefly on the surface before sinking out of sight.

Molly flexed her muscles and winced at the pain in her neck.

"Guys, it looks like we've got super powers," she said. "Powers that came to us in our dreams."

Buck, Georgie and Duffy nodded slowly.

Jackie jumped excitedly.

"Super powers?! No way?! What, what, WHAT about me?" he asked.

"You dreamed about biting things," said Molly. "So go bite something."

Jackie's head swiveled around as he looked for something fun to bite. He saw a huge old tree, let out a "YAP! YAP! YAP!" and ran over to it. But before he could start biting, nature called him. Jackie answered the call by lifting his leg and watering the base of the tree. He then bared his teeth and prepared to bite.

"No you dummy!" barked Georgie. "Not there!"

Jackie looked from Georgie to the wet spot on the tree.

He nodded and walked to the other side of the tree. The DRY side.

Jackie opened wide and chomped down on the tree's thick trunk. As he gnawed away, a blizzard of sawdust and wood chips flew around.

"Hey! HEY! Cut it out!" chirped a tweety voice that belonged to a very angry Cardinal who was hiding near the top of the tree. Jackie didn't hear the bird, as his ears were filled to overflowing with the sound of his teeth tearing through the wood.

He did feel it though when the Cardinal landed on his back and started pecking at his head.

"OUCH!" shrieked Jackie. "What's your, your, YOUR problem bird?!"

"Three things," chirped the Cardinal angrily. "One: this tree isn't a chew toy. It's my home."

"Oh" said Jackie. "Sorry, sorry, SORRY!!! I was just testing my teeth."

The Cardinal glanced at the base of the tree. It looked like a dozen hungry beavers had been having a wood buffet. He let out a low whistle.

"Your teeth seem to work just fine."

"What's the second thing?" asked Buck as he and the other Terriers arrived at the tree.

"My name isn't 'bird.' It's 'Sasquatch!'"

Molly stuck her big head right next to the Cardinal.

"My hearing isn't all that good," she said. "Was that 'Sasquatch'? Like 'Bigfoot'?"

The Cardinal known as "Sasquatch" hung his head. "Yeah, I really don't know what my parents were thinking."

Sasquatch was used to having birds and other creatures make fun of his name. It didn't mean that he enjoyed it though. So after listening to the Terriers giggle for about thirty seconds he fluttered towards their faces and chirped angrily at them.

"And the THIRD thing I have to say is that I don't know why you dogs are hanging out here when there's a gang of psycho-super-cats on the loose."

The Terriers stopped laughing.

"Did you say 'psycho-cats'?" asked Molly.

"No!" chirped Sasquatch. "I said 'psycho-SUPER-cats'. Five of them. They spent the morning climbing trees and attacking nests."

He pointed his red wing at a dozen nests that littered the ground. He then told the Terriers that the cats had really long claws that they used to climb the tallest trees in the park. Luckily, the local birds managed to escape...

"This time. But these cats look like they mean business. Especially the bald one."

"The only bald cat around here is that goon Patches," said Buck. "Looks like we know the cats that did this."

"But it doesn't make sense." said Georgie. "Since when did those cats have super claws?"

"And since when did WE have super powers?" asked Duffy.

"Oh! I know! I know! I FTHUI!!!" yapped Jackie as he spit a sliver out of his mouth. "We've had our powers since we woke up."

"Or maybe we had the powers before we went to sleep." Once again Molly had things figured out first.

Buck gave the Bull Terrier a questioning look. "What are you thinking Molly?"

"I have a theory" she began.

"What, what, what's a 'theory'?" asked Jackie.

Molly shook her head. "Just follow me."

She ran as fast as she could towards the site of the previous day's jerky feast. Which really wasn't all that fast. Getting old is a funny thing. Molly thought she was going so fast that the others would be struggling to keep up. In reality, they were jogging at a gentle pace and easily kept up with her.

Except for Duffy who really was pretty stumpy. And Sasquatch who was flying at half-speed a few feet above the dogs.

"Hey bird!" Georgie snapped up at the Cardinal. "Why are you following us?"

"Three more things," answered Sasquatch. "One: technically, I'm not 'following' you. I'm a little bit ahead of you. Two: with those cats on the loose, I feel safer hanging out with you guys. Three: since none of you 'super dogs' can fly, none of you can stop me from tagging along."

Sasquatch was about to add "so there," but he decided to hold his beak.

Molly slowed down even more as they arrived at the scene of the jerky feast. All of the boxes were empty. Sasquatch fluttered around, breathing in the aromas of the beef, bacon, chicken and turkey jerky. He let out a low whistle and muttered "Looks like there was a heck of a picnic here."

"It's ... just like... I thought..." panted Molly as she walked over to the empty boxes. "The cats must have ... eaten the ... cod jerky."

"Dumb cats!" laughed Duffy. "Even I wouldn't eat that."

"It all makes sense," Molly said, her breath now being almost fully caught. "We ate that jerky yesterday, and today we have super powers."

Buck was the next to figure it out. "So those cats ate the fish, and now they're climbing tall trees."

Georgie, Duffy and Jackie were confused. They looked from Buck to the jerky boxes and over to Molly. Slowly, they processed the facts. Then all at once they realized that the jerky had given them super powers. They didn't know that the meat was radioactive. That's not something that dogs worry about. They're more concerned with how food smells and tastes, and not whether it's going to alter their DNA and make them the strongest and most incredible dogs in the entire world.

"Awesome! That means we're the strongest and most incredible dogs in the world!" gloated Georgie.

Duffy's stomach growled angrily. "Do you think there's any of that jerky left?"

Sasquatch landed on one of the empty boxes. "There wouldn't have been a few pieces of worm jerky, would there?"

Molly shook her head.

"That's a drag," chirped Sasquatch. "Now what are you super dogs going to do about the psycho cats?"

The Terriers thought about it, but before they could come up with a plan, they heard a sound that propelled them into their first adventure as super heroes.

And that sound was...

EVER SEEN A FLYING DOG?

"WAAAAHHHH!!!"

Five Terriers and one bird turned towards the playground.

Duffy squinted and was able to see through hedges, a fence and a few other obstacles. His vision zoomed in and he saw Molly's small human Emma sitting and screaming at the top of her lungs.

"Bad news Molly!" he said. "It's Emma."

"She must need me!" shouted Molly as she took off at full speed.

Just then, another even louder voice rang out.

"WAAAAHHHH!!

Before Duffy could focus on the source of this screech, Jackie became agitated and started to bounce.

"I know that scream! It's my Jordana!" Jackie yelped. "Hold on! Hold on! HOLD ON!!!"

And with that, he took off at an even fuller speed than Molly.

Buck, Georgie and Duffy chased after Molly and Jackie. Sasquatch flew along too, and this time, the Terriers were too busy to try to shoo him away.

In the playground, Emma and Jordana were sitting by themselves and screaming as if every terrible thing you could imagine was happening to them.

Their screaming and crying didn't mean that they were in any danger. In this particular case, it meant that Emma wasn't allowed to chew on her Mother's sunglasses. Emma's cries made Jordana fussy. When that happened, she liked to stick her fingers in her Mother's hair.

Which is usually okay, but Nancy had just had her hair styled, and wasn't in the mood to throw away a nice hundred dollar hairdo to keep Jordana happy.

Her Mother's stern "No!" set Jordana off, and Nancy and Susan decided to give both girls a "time out." And the best spot for that was inside the dome-shaped set of monkey bars in the playground.

Which is where Emma and Jordana were sitting and screaming when the Terriers sprang into action.

As they approached the playground, Georgie decided to use her super power to help the girls. She unleashed a bark that was so piercingly loud, it made the other Terriers yelp in pain. The bark got louder as it reached the playground. The Mothers and Mrs. G. covered their ears just as the bark made their cell phones and a couple of juice boxes explode.

Unsure of what was going on, the Mothers decided to gather up their children and go home. But they never got the chance...

Usually, Buck prided himself on his ability to stay calm. Not this time. Fearing that Emma and Jordana were in danger, he took a deep breath, huffed, puffed and unleashed a cloud of mist. The cloud was then carried by a gust of wind towards the playground.

As soon as the mist reached the panicky Mothers and Mrs. G., it caused them to pass out.

It must be said that watching grownups collapse doesn't help to calm down screaming toddlers. It was at this point that Emma and Jordana REALLY began to wail.

"WAAAAHHHH!!

When Jackie reached the playground, he saw the Mothers and Mrs. G. passed out cold on the benches and on the ground. Nearby, Emma and Jordana were shrieking hysterically inside the monkey bars. It was up to Jackie to first free the children and then defeat whatever villain had locked them up.

"Jordana! Jordana!! JORDANA!!! I'll save you!" he yelped as he attacked the metal bars.

Just then, Buck, Duffy, Georgie and Sasquatch arrived. Being fairly perceptive, Buck quickly realized that there wasn't any danger in the park: it was his breath that knocked everyone out. Duffy agreed, adding that he knew enough about children to recognize a tantrum when he saw it.

Molly wasn't as calm. For as she arrived, all she saw was her beloved Emma sitting under the monkey bars crying as hard as she could. Summoning up her newly discovered super strength, Molly lowered her head and ran at full speed towards the monkey bars. Just then, having gnawed through one bar, Jackie's teeth chomped into a second.

"No! Wait!" yelled Buck, but Molly was too riled up to listen.

Molly hit the bars with the force of a rocket-powered bulldozer and the climbing apparatus was flung off of the girls. Unfortunately, Jackie was still gnawing away and he was shot up into the air along with the monkey bars.

"Maybe you guys CAN fly." Sasquatch chirped in amazement.

Emma and Jordana watched the monkey bars and Jackie as they soared across the playground. Neither of them had ever seen a flying dog, and the sight was so funny that they quickly forgot their tantrums and began to laugh.

Buck, Georgie and Duffy couldn't bear to see Jackie crash to the ground. As they turned away, they saw that the humans were waking up.

The Mothers and Mrs. G. were understandably confused as they saw Buck, Georgie and Duffy. They were even more confused by the set of monkey bars that was lying upside down on the other side of the field. Before they could get worried about the girls, they saw Molly walking towards them with smiling Emma riding on her back. Just behind them, Jordana toddled along with a very dizzy and slightly stunned Jackie.

"What just happened?" asked Nancy.

It was a question that none of the other humans could answer. The Terriers knew, but even if they were going to tell the humans, and even if the humans could understand what they were saying... well, they just never would have believed it.

As Emma climbed down, Molly turned to face the other Terriers.

"We need to have a talk about using our powers properly." She said this approximately two seconds before her tired legs gave out and she fell to the ground.

WHO PUT THAT POODLE THERE?

The next day, Molly was too stiff and sore to go to the park. A full day of resting in the backyard sun would definitely help her joints and muscles recover. Just as she was getting comfortable however, a loud "CHEEP!" woke her up.

Molly opened her eyes and saw Sasquatch waving his wings frantically.

"The guys are waiting for you!"

"Tell them we'll have our talk tomorrow."

Sasquatch hopped onto Molly's side. "No! They need you now. They say you have to see what the cats have done."

Molly knew that she had to get up. The neighborhood's safety was more important than her sore legs. With a deep sigh and a mighty groan, Molly stood and slowly headed out.

Even before she met up with her friends, Molly could smell that something was wrong. She sniffed and caught a whiff of the other Terriers, and the lingering aroma of Peter's cat posse. But there was something else in the air: the smell of fear. And of Miniature Poodle.

It was an awful stench, and Molly wondered why the park smelled like scared Poodle. The mystery lasted until she rounded the corner and saw... a scared Poodle.

Poodles are just about the most neurotic animals around. And the smaller the Poodle, the larger its storehouse of nervousness. So when a really small Poodle is stuck to a wall ten feet off the ground, its level of anxiety is right off the charts.

The Poodle on the wall was named "Baby," and he was probably the most annoying dog in the neighborhood. Baby was a twitchy, bony bundle of nerves who yapped at Molly every time she walked by. If Molly ever barked back at Baby, he would screech like a cat and act like he'd been threatened.

None of the other Terriers liked Baby and would normally cross the road to avoid him. However, the canine code of honor required them to help a dog in need. And at the moment, Baby had a near record-setting amount of need.

As Molly arrived, Buck, Georgie, Duffy and Jackie were trying to get Baby to relax. Since this was a dog who freaked out when he heard the toilet flush, being stuck on a wall high above the ground put him WAY past the point where he could be calmed down

"How did this happen?" asked Molly.

"Poodle said it was the cats," answered Buck.

The Terriers exchanged a look of disgust. In their minds, no self-respecting dog would let a cat, or even a bunch of cats, get the better of it.

Baby saw the look and spoke up to defend himself.

"It's not my fault," he began. "The cats have super strength or something! They cornered me and rubbed against me. Next thing I know, Peter and Patches were carrying me up this wall."

With that, Baby began to sob like a... well, like a baby.

The Terriers exchanged another glance. This time, it was a look of concern that passed between them. Now they knew that the cats had at least a couple of super powers. They had extra-long claws that allowed them to climb walls and tall trees, and apparently their fur could now produce huge amounts of static electricity. At least enough to keep a miniature

Poodle stuck to a wall for, say... hmmm... about...

"Hey! Hey! Hey! Baby! How long have you been up there?" asked Jackie.

"At least three pees," answered Baby.

"So," figured Molly, "he's been there since first thing this morning."

Which made sense, because cats always get up to mischief like ripping open garbage bags and terrorizing birds in the wee small hours when humans are asleep and unable to see them acting badly.

"The cats told me to tell you that this is a warning," whimpered Baby. "They said that if you Terriers get in their way, no one will be safe."

Suddenly, it began to rain around the Terriers.

"He's now been here for four pees," said Georgie.

Not wanting to stick around for a fifth pee, the Terriers tried to figure out how to get Baby down. As none of them had taken a science or engineering class, they could only guess at the best way to do it.

Georgie thought that she could use a couple of super barks to knock the wall over. Molly and Buck didn't think this was a very smart idea. After all, Baby could be crushed by the collapsing wall. But as is often the case with Westies, Georgie didn't listen to reason. Instead, she took a deep breath and let loose a tremendous bark. Georgie's noise echoed around the park and bounced back with extra force. The sound waves didn't knock down the wall, but they did shatter the windows near Baby.

As the Terriers dodged the falling glass, Baby squirmed and cried even louder.

"I'm losing the feeling in my paws," he whimpered.

Molly shook her head and spoke firmly to the Terriers.

"This is exactly why we need to work on our super powers. If we can't control them, they are completely useless."

Buck nodded slowly. "You're right. Practice will start soon as we get that dust mop off of the wall."

Duffy growled up at Baby. "I say we leave him up there. Let the vultures get him!"

"No can do Duff. We gotta help our fellow dog," said Buck as he stepped towards the wall.

He puckered his lips and whistled out a stream of mist. The mist floated into the bricks behind Baby and cut through them like a laser beam. Baby's eyes popped in terror as the bricks melted.

He didn't get a chance to squeal as he plummeted to the ground and crashed heavily in front of the Terriers.

"OWWWW!!!" he howled.

"You know," said Sasquatch, "you guys really should have caught him."

All five Terriers shrugged in unison as Baby struggled to his feet and staggered away. The distressed Poodle shook off the bits of brick that still clung to his fur. He then looked at the Terriers who were giggling and smirking at him. They may have saved his life, but there was no way that Baby would ever thank them. Instead, he tried to look tough and dignified as he slowly limped away from the school.

Sasquatch was right; catching Baby would have been the right thing to do. But if he and the Terriers knew what Baby was soon going to do, they would never have helped him off of the wall.

A SUPER HERO BONDING RITUAL

After the great poodle rescue, it was time for the Terriers to practice their powers and figure out what they could and couldn't do.

Georgie asked Molly if she could use her bark to knock the doors off of Mrs. G.'s cupboards. That way, she could get at the huge box of treats that Mrs. G. brought home the other day.

Molly shook her head.

"But I'd share!" Georgie protested. "And they smell SOOO good."

Molly was firm. If the Terriers used their powers for selfish things like stealing treats, then they'd surely end up getting in trouble. Even worse, the humans would find out about their powers. Unlike dogs, humans act in weird and unpredictable ways. There'd be no telling what they'd do if they found out that their family pets had super powers. It was a risk that the Terriers didn't feel like taking.

"Remember," pointed out Molly, "one of the reasons our humans love us is that they think we're helpless without them."

The Terriers understood this, but Sasquatch was shocked.

"You mean to say that dogs play dumb around humans?"

"No, no, NO!" yipped Jackie. "Not all of us. At least not <u>all the</u> time"

"Some dogs don't play dumb, they <u>are</u> dumb." Buck said as he pointed at Baby who could still be seen in the distance staring at his tail.

"Also," said Molly, "we should only use our powers for the good of our neighborhood."

The Terriers looked serious as they nodded. They loved their neighborhood. It was full of great smells. Their families lived here, as did their best friends. They would do anything to keep it safe.

After a short discussion, the Terriers agreed to the following rules:
1. They had to perfect their super powers.
2. Their powers had to be kept hidden from the humans!
3. Their powers could only be used for the good of the neighborhood!!
4. Their powers could only be used when absolutely necessary!!!

The Terriers were now more than just friends: they were joined together in a secret club. A club that they felt needed a catchy name. After considering "Doers of Good" or "D.O.G." and the "Helpful Organization of UNited Dogs" or "H.O.U.ND." and "Super Terriers United to Foil Fiends" or "S.T.U.F.F." they decided to go with "Super Powerful Organization of Terriers" which they shortened to "S.P.O.T."

It may not have been perfect, but it was a lot better than Jackie's suggestion of the "Neighborhood Union of TerrierS" or "N.U.TS"

They now had their powers, their rules, a name for their group, and they even had a team of evil feline archenemies. All that was left for them to do before they became an official legion of super heroes was to create a secret bonding ritual. With that in mind, Molly held out a fore paw.

"We are the Super Terriers!" she began. "Molly! The power of super strength!"

Buck put his paw on top of Molly's and barked out "Buck! The power of super breath!"

Jackie had to stand on his hind legs to get his paw on top of Buck's.

"Jackie! The power of super, super, SUPER chewing!"

Georgie struggled up on her hind legs and put a paw on top of the others'. Unfortunately, she lost her balance and her face smacked against Jackie's paw.

"Owww! You need to get your nails trimmed." Georgie snapped.

(Just a thought here. When a dog gets its nails trimmed, is it called a "peticure?")

"My nails are fine, fine, FINE!" yipped Jackie.

"Shush!" ordered Molly. "Teammates don't fight!"

With that, Molly lay down and put her paw on the ground. Buck followed her lead and put his paw on top. Jackie and then Georgie did the same.

"Georgie! The power of super barking."

Duffy's stumpy paw joined the others.

"Duffy! The power of super eye sight."

The others shook their heads.

"You can't call it 'super eye sight'" said Georgie.

"Really?!" barked Duffy angrily, "WHY NOT?!"

While no Terrier likes being told what to do, Duffy really hated it. He tried his best to look defiant and intimidating, but even his best friends had trouble taking him seriously at times like this. It might have been the fact that he became upset so easily... or it might have been his poofy hair.

"Why can't I use the slogan that I like?" growled Duffy defiantly.

"Because it sounds lame," said Buck in a firm, steady voice that made Duffy start to consider backing down.

"Try 'super vision'," suggested Molly.

The other Terriers nodded. Duffy also thought it sounded good, but he had to save face. After a few moments of huffing and growling Duffy agreed that "super vision" was the best way to describe his power. He then suggested that the gang join paws to reaffirm their unity.

Thus, the Super Powerful Organization of Terriers was formed. From that day forth, the neighborhood would be protected by a group of feisty dogs dedicated to justice, safety and the pursuit of all things cat and rodent-like.

A SUPER HERO BONDING RITUAL – TAKE 2

"Wait a second!" squawked Sasquatch. "What about me? I'm a part of this group!"

The Terriers stared at the Cardinal.

Duffy had calmed down enough to say something that everyone knew: "But you're not a Terrier. You're a bird."

"And <u>we</u> have super powers," added Georgie. "No offense, but we don't need you."

Sasquatch flapped his wings angrily as he hovered a few inches off the ground.

"So Miss Super Powerful Dog, tell me something; can any of you fly?"

The Terriers looked at each other as they had the same thought.

So they tried to fly. And they tried. And they tried again. And each time, they failed miserably. Duffy and Molly could barely get their feet off the ground. The closest any of them came was Jackie who could jump twice his height into the air. Impressive for a dog, but you couldn't call it "flying." In fact, you couldn't even call it "taking off."

Terriers are strong-willed dogs, so after catching their breath, and despite the overwhelming evidence that they could not, in fact, fly... they tried once again. And once again, they failed miserably. They finally had to admit that despite all of their awesome new powers, flying was something that they just couldn't do.

"Big deal," growled Georgie. "Flying isn't so great anyway."

"Oh really?" taunted Sasquatch as he flew circles around the Terriers. "It comes in pretty handy for me."

"Bird's got a point," said Buck as he looked over to Molly.

The old Bull Terrier agreed and told the others that Sasquatch could be a great help to the team. He could help keep an eye on the neighborhood, and would be able to see things that the dogs couldn't.

With that, Molly and then Buck put out their paws. Jackie smiled at Sasquatch as he put his paw on top of Buck's. Georgie and Duffy sighed unhappily, but they joined in the team paw session.

Sasquatch flew over and landed on top of the paws.

"Congratulations," said Molly. "You are now an honorary Terrier."

The little Cardinal's chest puffed out proudly. "Thanks for letting me join 'S.P.O.T.S.'"

"What the heck is 'S.P.O.T.S.?'" demanded Duffy.

"You know, the 'Super Powerful Organization of Terriers and Songbird'."

Georgie and Duffy pulled away their paws and Sasquatch fell to the ground.

"No way!" barked Duffy. "We want a name that will scare our enemies. And no one is afraid of a small bird."

Georgie laughed and pretended to be a cat.

"Oh! I am just so scared!" she hissed. "The gang from S.P.O.T.S. is going to chirp so loudly at us!"

Up until this moment, Sasquatch had been willing to turn the other beak when the Terriers - and specifically Georgie and Duffy - were rude to him. But this, this was too much for a proud bird to take.

"That's it!" he squawked. "I'm out of here!"

As is often the case when animals or people get mad, Sasquatch didn't really mean what he said. He was just waiting for an apology. This came almost immediately from Molly who was older and much, much wiser than her hotheaded friends Georgie and Duffy.

"Calm down Sasquatch." Molly said. "They're just teasing."

Molly looked at Georgie and Duffy who didn't look like they were "just teasing." Molly stood up straight and tried to look intimidating.

"WEREN'T you guys?"

Georgie and Duffy took a step back from Molly and pretended to be sorry.

"That's right." Grumbled Georgie.

"Just teasing..." mumbled Duffy.

Molly looked from the Westie to the Dandy Dinmont and then over to the Cardinal. None of them seemed too happy, but Molly was satisfied that Sasquatch wasn't going to leave.

"Good," she said. "Because we have work to do. Remember, the cats also have super powers. I don't know what they're doing right now, but I don't think they're fighting with each other."

HAIRBALLS

Molly was right; the cats weren't fighting or arguing. Instead, they were working together to perfect their powers.

After eating the fishy cod jerky, the cats found themselves in possession of a number of powers. But unlike the dogs, all five of the cats had the same super powers.

This happened because cats are more or less all the same. Sure, they may look different from each other, but they tend to do the same few things. Sleep, drink milk, claw the corner of a couch, use the litter box, lick themselves, eat and go back to sleep.

Compare that to dogs, each and every one of whom has a unique personality. They may share traits with other dogs, and habits with other members of their breed, but each dog is different. Some are friendlier than others, some are more active than others, and some are smarter than others. But they are all different.

That's why each of the Terriers had a single, unique skill, while the cats all had the same powers.

This did not however, work to the dogs' advantage. Because Peter, Petunia, Puss Puss, Precious and that goon Patches each had four super powers. Their claws were super long and sharp enough to allow the cats to climb almost any surface. And as Baby the whiny Poodle had found out, the cats' fur was now able to produce huge amounts of static electricity.

The cats could also stretch out their tongues until they were about three feet long. The rough barbs on their tongues became huge and were so rough that the cats could use them like industrial-grade sandpaper to grind down hard surfaces like walls, doors or, as Patches threatened, "dog's heads."

Their last power was the ability to vomit up and shoot hair balls with great force. Feel free to say "yecch!", "blecch!", "fooey!" or any other word that means that something is really disgusting. Because that just may be the most repulsive super power ever.

To find the gang of cats, we have to travel to the other side of the neighborhood, all the way to the big old abandoned home with its weed-filled back yard. This deserted mansion had recently become the headquarters of F.U.S.S. which was the name that Peter had created for the cats. It stood for "Felines United in Selfish Service." Even though none of the other cats liked the name, Peter told them that it wasn't up for discussion; he had chosen the name, and it wouldn't be changing.

"Ever!"

Inside the house, the floors were covered with plaster that the cats had shredded off the walls. The doors of the kitchen cupboards had been yanked off by the cats' tongues, and the wallpaper throughout the house had been rubbed by static electricity-charged fur until it curled up in strips. As a result, the walls looked like a head full of frizzy hair. If, that is, that particular head was completely flat and the hair looked like colored vinyl wallpaper with dried glue hanging off of it. Which is to say that this comparison isn't all that good. So, just imagine then that curled up strips of wallpaper were all over the walls. It's much simpler and really, it's much more accurate.

The tour of "F.U.S.S. Central" will now move on to the basement where a pitiful, pathetic poodle was in real trouble.

"Help!" whined Baby whose pleading was met with a "THWACK!"

"No! Please!"

"THWACK!"

"Stop it!"

"THWACK!"

Baby shook in fear and trembled with disgust as he desperately tried to evade the hairballs that the cats were shooting at him. Or was he trembling with fear and shaking in disgust? Not much difference really, but his reactions to his surroundings made perfect sense as all around him were oozing, dripping hairy projectiles from inside a cat's belly.

"Y-y-you said I could go home!" Baby wailed.

"Did I?" asked Peter. "I gueth I lied. Puth Puth! Fire!"

Puss Puss looked at Baby and gauged the exact distance between himself and the dog. He was busy calculating which angle to release the hairball from as well as the force that he needed to use when he heard...

"THWACK!" as a hairball - actually, it didn't really look like a ball; it was more like a huge gooey kidney bean - whizzed past Baby's face and stuck on the wall.

"Who did that?!" demanded Puss Puss who had been mere seconds away from unloading his regurgitated missile.

"Me!" hissed Petunia. "You was taking too long."

As Baby tried to quietly sneak away, Puss Puss turned on Petunia.

"I was simply trying to get the perfect aim you thug! If you'd have put some thought into your shot, you might have actually hit that thing!"

Petunia was the type of cat that would never slink away from a fight. So there was no way he'd let an egghead intimidate him.

"So maybe you can learn me how to do it, Professor," he snarled.

Puss Puss was working on a smart response when he noticed that Baby was sneaking towards the stairs. The Poodle was just starting to imagine that he might be able to escape further pain and humiliation when SPLAT!!! He was hit. The force of Puss Puss' expectoration knocked Baby over and sent him skidding away from the stairs.

Petunia nodded at Puss Puss. Maybe aiming was a good idea after all.

"You promised!" squealed Baby as he weakly got to his feet. "You were going to let me go home if I told you about the Terriers and their powers. Remember?! And where's that bone you said I could have?"

"Here's a lesson for you dog," purred Patches. "Never trust a cat."

Tears formed in Baby's eyes. It was bad enough that he'd betrayed members of his own species. To him, it was even worse that instead of getting a juicy, fatty steak bone, his reward was to become target practice for the cats. Baby's sniveling and sniffling sounded truly wretched. If cats weren't such heartless beasts, they just might have felt sorry for him. But they are, so they didn't.

Luckily for Baby, the cat gang was tired. Peter had been making them practice for hours.

"Maybe we should let him go," meowed Precious. "My poor tummy is starting to hurt."

Peter was about to arch his back and spit, when he noticed that all the cats looked like they'd had enough hairball shooting practice for the day.

"Perhapth you're right." Peter nodded.

"WAIT!" Yowled Patches in sadistic glee. "Make him run the gauntlet!"

"No!" squealed Baby.

"Yeth!" hissed Peter happily.

The other cats smiled, nodded and began to regurgitate. Baby had just a couple of seconds to try to climb the stairs. Unfortunately, he wasn't a racing dog like a Whippet. He was just a small poodle and had only made it up three stairs before the hairballs began to fly fast and hard.

There's no need for the sickening details of what happened next. Let's just say that by the time Baby escaped, he was bruised, soggy, battered and completely disgusted.

Moments later, Peter led the cats out of the house. He was purring out a mixture of happiness and excitement.

"At thith rate, we'll be in control of the neighborhood in no time."

He then began what was meant to be an evil laugh. But a full afternoon of hairball-shooting had left his throat feeling sore and phlegmy. Instead of a scare-inducing cackle, Peter launched into a coughing fit.

The other cats also tried to laugh menacingly, but their throats were in a similar state as Peter's. So what was meant to be a chorus of evil laughter quickly became a cacophony of coughs and gasps.

But they were EVIL coughs and gasps.

HEROES IN TRAINING

As the cats from "F.U.S.S." struggled to catch their breaths, the dogs from "S.P.O.T.S." were busy honing their powers.

Sasquatch's first task as an "Honorary Terrier" was to help Georgie and Duffy work on their super skills. Both dogs said that they didn't need help from a bird, but Molly insisted. She figured that if Georgie and Duffy worked with Sasquatch, they might eventually welcome him to the team.

Once again, Molly was right. Sasquatch quickly proved himself to the cranky Terriers.

It wasn't easy though. Like all Westies, Georgie suffered from a nasty case of stubbornness. Once she'd insulted Sasquatch, she found it difficult to change the way she spoke to him.

Sasquatch ignored Georgie's hardheadedness and tried to find a way to get her to focus her barking. This he did by using his beak to rip open the bags full of recyclable materials that Mrs. G. left in the back yard. Georgie was worried that Mrs. G. would get mad at her, but Sasquatch shredded the bags to make it look like a raccoon had vandalized them.

Georgie smiled as she realized that this would make Mrs. G. really mad at the raccoons that lived in her trees. So mad, that she just might call a pest control guy to get rid of them.

By "get rid of," Georgie didn't mean "exterminated" or anything like that. No. Mrs. G. wasn't that mean. Instead, Georgie was merely hoping that she'd arrange for a "humane" animal control guy to capture the raccoons and take them out to the country where they could live happily in nature.

Until they were eaten by bears.

Hey - it may not be nice, but that's how dogs think.

One of the many reasons that dogs are "man's best friend" is that they ALL hate raccoons. The smallest, most spoiled Teacup Terrier or Chihuahua, the type of pets that are happy to wear the sparkly collars and colorful sweaters that their humans have bought for them, will act like a hungry Doberman when it senses a raccoon in the area. Even those toy-like dogs understand that raccoons are horrible, awful creatures that give all mammals a bad name.

Harsh? Maybe.

But true? Absolutely.

After Sasquatch made it look like raccoons that had torn apart Mrs. G.'s garbage bags, he and Georgie dragged out empty bottles and cans and set them up all over the backyard.

Sasquatch fluttered around the yard and chirped out target bottles and cans for Georgie to bark at. At first, Georgie's explosive WOOFS!! blew up three or four bottles at a time. But it didn't take too long for Sasquatch to get Georgie to properly aim her powerful yaps and yelps. Within a few hours, the Westie's barks were focussed enough to pierce small, precisely formed holes in cans and bottles.

Georgie was pleased with her newly perfected super power. She was also happy about the way Sasquatch had framed the local raccoons. For the first time, Georgie smiled at Sasquatch. She wanted to thank the bird, but was having trouble forming the words. Sasquatch smiled at Georgie and nodded his tiny head in understanding.

"Don't mention it," he cheeped. "That's what team mates are for."

Sasquatch was smiling as he flew to Duffy's house where he helped him perfect his super vision by playing a new style of "hide and seek." In this version, the "seeker" - Duffy - stayed in his backyard while the "hider" - Sasquatch - travelled further and further away. As soon as Duffy could see where the Cardinal was hiding, he would bark as loudly as he could. The game ended when Sasquatch was too far away to hear Duffy's bark. This didn't occur until Sasquatch was hiding behind the sign at a gas station which was at least a 10 minute walk away.

Like Georgie, Duffy appreciated Sasquatch's help. But unlike Georgie, he didn't even try to thank the Cardinal. It didn't matter though. The mere fact that Duffy was no longer baring his teeth told Sasquatch that they'd now be able to work together without any fussing or fighting.

While Sasquatch was busy training Georgie and Duffy, Buck was experimenting with his super breath. He'd already learned how to focus his blasts by puckering his lips when he exhaled. He also discovered that different foods caused his breath to possess different powers. His usual diet of kibble gave him mild gas which created breath that could dissolve solid objects. His "treat" meal of canned wet food created a different type of gas that led to breath that could slice through almost any object. Kind of like a dog-breath laser. And when Buck was given a cookie treat, his breath blasts were strong enough to make any target explode.

After making this discovery, Buck put his cookie breath to what he felt was good use by blowing up all the squirrel nests that he could see. Messy noisy fun, and something that most dogs would do if they could.

Meanwhile, Jackie's self-training was going really well. This may surprise those people and dogs who don't think of Jack Russell Terriers as being among the brightest of the breeds.

Are they energetic? Absolutely. Are they loyal? For sure. Are they funny? A lot of the time. Are they smart? Well, let's just say that most people, as well as members of most other breeds, think of Russells as the types of dogs that will often chase their own tails.

Yet Jackie showed a great deal of intelligence when it came to perfecting his Super Gnawing power. He remembered that when he was teething, he had chewed up the legs of the dining room table.

And the legs of the couch.

And three pairs of sneakers ... an umbrella... a football... a water bowl... a doll...

And many, many other things.

He was repeatedly warned to stop and was even threatened with a rolled up newspaper. Jackie didn't like that newspaper and he shredded it when his humans weren't around. When he finished the paper, he got right back to chewing everything in the house. Jackie's chewing of non-edible objects ended after he destroyed a wallet which held a driver's license, an important receipt and eighty-seven dollars. This time, Jackie's large human Mike used a rolled up magazine to swat his butt.

It didn't hurt; it just kind of stung for a few seconds. What really upset Jackie was the look of disappointment on his friend Mike's face. Despite what a lot of people think, dogs are able to understand something called "cause and effect." That's how Jackie came to realize that Mike's unhappiness was caused by his chewing of the wallet.

And that's when Jackie vowed never to chew anything in the house except for his many, many toys.

So that's why he didn't practice his super gnawing <u>inside</u> the house. Which is why the fence in the backyard was soon riddled with holes. Luckily for Jackie, none of his human friends would ever think that he could chew through a chain link fence.

Or a cement garden gnome.

Or even the old bike that was gathering weeds in the corner of the yard.

Jackie may have been smart in how he trained, but Molly was absolutely brilliant. She had already learned that using her super strength tired her out and made her muscles ache. She wisely concluded that the best way for her to build up her strength would be to put on some weight for extra padding. Every dog knows that the best way to bulk up is to sit by the dinner table and smile an extra cute smile while the family is eating. This works especially well with kids. It also works when the meal smells kind of burned and even the grown-ups don't want to eat it.

The food wasn't always tasty, but Molly ate and ate. Soon she was chunkier than she had ever been.

With their training complete, the Terriers were ready to stand on guard as the protectors of the neighborhood. Which was a good thing, because the cats from F.U.S.S. were about to take their villainy to the next level. And they were going to do it soon...

HOW TO WAKE A TERRIER

It hadn't taken Peter long to create a plan that was so diabolical and so ambitious that it would leave no doubt as to which animals were in control of the neighborhood.

The night of the launch of the cats' reign of terror was clear and calm. Luckily for the neighborhood, it was a perfect night for birds of prey to be out hunting mice. You see, a few minutes past midnight, an owl buddy of Sasquatch's was gliding over the area looking for small rodents for a late night snack. That's when he saw something that made him "HOOT!" in amazement. Eight raccoons and six skunks were marching in formation behind Peter and the cats from F.U.S.S.

The Owl could tell that the cats and their cronies were up to no good, so he flew over to Sasquatch's nest to tell him what he'd seen. Sasquatch thanked the Owl and asked if he wanted to join S.P.O.T.S. in their fight to protect the neighborhood.

The Owl shook his head, which is quite a sight because owls can turn their heads nearly completely around.

"I'm way too hungry to fight," said the Owl.

Sasquatch understood and thanked the Owl by telling him where he'd seen a few fat, slow mice. He then flew to Molly's house.

Sasquatch knew that Molly was the wisest of the Super Terriers. He also knew that she was the leader of the gang. But what Sasquatch did not yet understand was that Molly was hard of hearing. So as he tapped on the window above Molly's bed, he couldn't figure out why she didn't wake up.

He knew that she wasn't dead, as he could see her rolling around in her sleep. Yet even though Sasquatch tapped harder and harder on the glass, Molly showed no sign of responding.

Sasquatch had a decision to make. He could stay at the window, and tap away on the glass until his beak was worn down to a nub, or he could move on and try to wake up one of the other Terriers.

Wisely, Sasquatch chose the second option. He shook his head at the snoozing - and to be honest, the drooling - Molly, and flew off to Jackie's house. He landed on the mailbox and quietly peeped "Jackie." A split-second later, he heard Jackie running full speed through the house.

"That dog is a REALLY light sleeper," thought Sasquatch.

A moment later, Jackie chewed a small hole in the front door and ran to Sasquatch who told him that the cats were up to something.

"And it sounds big."

"Let's get the others! Now! Now!! NOW!!!" yipped Jackie.

As Jackie ran towards Buck's house, Sasquatch flew next to him and repeated what the owl had said. With each word chirped in his ear, Jackie became more anxious and ran faster and faster. In fact, he became so frantic that he couldn't think clearly. Which would explain why he ran past Buck's house and kept right on running.

"Dogs!" chirped Sasquatch as he fluttered towards a tree in Buck's backyard.

After landing on one of the tree's lower branches, Sasquatch saw that Buck was sitting on a couch watching TV with his teenaged human Mark. Sasquatch thought that this was strange, but never having lived in a house with teenagers, he had no idea about the late hours that they often kept. Like all birds, Sasquatch avoided humans as if they were cats. But since the actual cats were planning something that was probably really big and really bad, there was no choice: he simply had to make his presence known.

Sasquatch took a deep breath, jumped off the branch and braced himself for impact as he flew into the screen door next to the couch. Since Cardinals only weigh a few ounces (or if you prefer using the metric system - a few dozen grams), Sasquatch's impact with the screen wasn't all that loud... for Buck and Mark that is.

But for Sasquatch, the collision was very, very noisy indeed. To him, it sounded like a truck driving into the side of a mountain that was made out of glass... and the glass mountain was an inch from Sasquatch's head.

Despite the noise that echoed in Sasquatch's brain, neither Buck nor Mark took their eyes off of the TV. Sasquatch tried to ignore the throbbing in his head as he tapped on the glass door. This time Buck looked towards him. But before he could come over to investigate, Mark began to scratch him behind the ears. This must have been Buck's "happy spot," because as soon as the scratching started, Buck collapsed on Mark's lap with a blissful look on his face.

For the second time in just a few minutes, Sasquatch muttered "Dogs!" and thought how much easier this mission would be if birds had found the super jerky. But it was the Terriers who were super powered, and with the neighborhood in danger, Sasquatch couldn't just let the dogs be dogs. He had to get them together to fight the cats and their vermin allies. Time was wasting, and even though Buck looked like he was having the time of his life, Sasquatch knew that he had to act.

"BUCK! GET OUT HERE!" he squawked.

Buck heard Sasquatch and immediately jumped up and growled.

"What's up Buck?" asked Mark.

By the way he was looking at his dog, it seemed as if Mark was expecting an answer in English.

Instead of answering in English, Spanish, French or even Urdu, Buck walked to the window and scanned the back yard. He didn't have to look long or far to see Sasquatch flapping his wings like a hummingbird. In bird sign language, this gesture means "Hurry up! The cats are on a rampage!"

Unfortunately, as was the case with Spanish, French and Urdu, Buck didn't understand bird sign language. But as a Terrier, Buck was fluent in the language of high strung agitation. Thinking quickly, Buck turned to Mark and let out his most pathetic "please let me out or else I'll mess up the carpet" whinny.

Mark slid open the door and told Buck not to run too far. His show was almost over and he had to start doing his homework.

Buck loved his family members, but like most Terriers, he felt free to ignore a majority of what they said. Sure enough, as soon as Buck was outside, he ran over to Sasquatch who was frantically chirping about the cats. One of them flew and the other one ran out of the backyard as Mark looked on in surprise.

Mark would have yelled at Buck to stop, but that might have woken up his Mom who would then have yelled at him to turn off the TV and get to bed. He would then have to tell her that he still had homework to do, which would have made her really angry and might have led to his being forbidden to watch TV for an extended period of time. With the playoffs starting the next night, Mark couldn't take that risk. So he slid the door shut and just hoped that Buck would come home soon.

He then went back to the couch to watch the end of his show.

Buck and Sasquatch were barely halfway to Georgie's house when Jackie and Duffy ran up to them. Duffy explained that he'd heard Jackie barking, so he used his super vision to look through the wall and saw him running in circles in the middle of the road. Luckily, Duffy's family had a Dandy Dinmont-sized doggie gate cut into their back door, so getting out was easy. Getting Jackie to calm down enough to tell him what was wrong took a bit longer.

The three Terriers and Sasquatch rushed to Georgie's place. Since Mrs. G. was very hard of hearing, they knew that they could be loud. So Buck, Duffy and Jackie began to bark their heads off. Well, that's not literally true, because without their heads, they wouldn't be able to continue their mission. Sasquatch joined the noisemaking by singing one of his favorite Cardinal songs. The song was called "Hey! Look At Me!" and like most bird songs, its lyrics are very simple.

HEY! LOOK AT ME!
Music: Traditional, Lyrics: Pretty Red
"Hey! Hey!
Hey! Hey!
Hey! Hey!
Look! Look!
Look at me!
I'm a pretty cardinal!
Hey! Hey!"

Georgie must have been in a deep sleep, because by the time she jumped off of the bed to see what was causing the commotion, some of Mrs. G's neighbors were yelling at the dogs and the Cardinal.

When she saw her friends and Sasquatch, Georgie knew that she had to get out of the house and join them. She was about to let out a door-shattering bark when Buck gestured for her to stop. With the neighbors threatening to call Animal

Control (a.k.a. "The Dog Catchers"), he realized that they had to free Georgie in as quiet a way as possible. Luckily for everyone, Mark had given Buck a full bowl of his favorite wet food.

"Step back!" he ordered as he flexed his stomach muscles. Buck could feel the air and gas bubbles working their way up his digestive tract. He stepped towards the front door, puckered up and let out a laser-thin blast of super breath.

As Buck's breath sliced a doggy portal in Mrs. G.'s door, Duffy and Jackie smelled something that made their tails wag.

"Your breath smells great, great, GREAT!" yipped Jackie.

Buck shut down his laser breath to tell Jackie to "shush!"

Duffy knew he should be quiet, but his mouth was watering, and he just had to know...

"What'd you eat?" he whispered.

"Turducken." Answered Buck. "Turkey, duck and chicken."

Jackie and Duffy's jaws dropped.

"And ... and... and..." Jackie was so excited that he had trouble keeping his voice down. "It's ALL mixed together?"

Buck nodded.

"Whoooaaaaa..." drool began to drip off Jackie and Duffy's tongues.

Buck smiled. "Yeah, it's really good."

The three of them shared a quiet moment thinking about Turducken. They would have shared a few hours thinking about it if Sasquatch hadn't squawked angrily at them.

"Forget about his dinner! The neighborhood's in danger!"

Buck nodded and puckered up to finish laser-breathing the door. When he was done, Georgie squeezed out of the hole and ran past her friends.

"What are you doing?" asked the increasingly frantic Sasquatch.

"What's it look like I'm doing?!" snapped back Georgie who was at that very moment squatting as she sprinkled all over a dead patch of grass.

Once again, Sasquatch rolled his little birdie eyes and sighed "Dogs..."

The other dogs gave Georgie the details as she finished her business. By the time she had wiped her paws and flung bits of sod all over the place, she was as angry as a West Highland Terrier could be. Which, if you've ever seen a mad Westie, is pretty angry indeed.

"Now," Georgie snarled, "let's show those cats who really runs the neighborhood."

She then growled so deeply and menacingly, that you'd have thought the noise came from a Mastiff or a Great Dane.

Before Georgie could harness her rage and take on the cats, she and the others had to get their leader. As they ran and flew to Molly's house, it was decided that

Georgie was the only one capable of making a noise that would be loud enough to wake her. Georgie was so fired up that she began unleashing super barks well before they arrived at Molly's house.

The barks were loud enough to wake people all over the neighborhood. The deep sleepers who weren't disturbed by Georgie's barks were woken by the car and house alarms set off by their low rumbling vibrations.

Over at Molly's house, the super bark caused baby Aaron to start shrieking, while Emma began to giggle. Aaron's screeching woke up Susan who came running into his room.

The last one up was Molly, and it wasn't Georgie's sonic-boom barks that woke her. It was the vibrations of Susan's panicked footsteps. Molly woke up and immediately started barking "Are you okay? Are you okay?" to her family. Once Susan realized that Aaron was all right, she told her husband Nick to take the dog to see what was going on outside.

Nick ran down the stairs and nearly tripped over Molly who was trying to run upstairs.

"Come on girl!" he yelled playfully and dramatically. "It's go time!"

Nick flung open the front door, and saw that at least one light was on in most of the houses on the street. In many cases, an angry neighbor was leaning out of a window or standing by a front door, trying to turn off their car's alarm with their electronic keys. As Nick walked across the road to talk to his neighbors, Molly saw Buck, Georgie, Duffy and Jackie trying to hide behind some bushes. Sasquatch was perched on top of the hedge waving frantically for her to come over.

Molly made sure that Nick wasn't watching before barreling over to the other members of S.P.O.T.S.

"We've got a situation," whispered Duffy. "A really bad situation."

HOW TO BARGAIN WITH
A SQUIRREL

"What's going on with the humans?" asked Molly as she pointed at the men and women who were trying to turn off their alarms.

"It's not about them," answered Buck.

"It's about the cats!" yipped Jackie. "The cats! The cats are going crazy!"

"Yeah! Them and their slimy raccoon and skunk buddies," sneered Georgie.

Molly tensed up at the mention of "skunks" and "raccoons." When she was a pup, she had her share of battles with skunks. She just couldn't resist chasing them. As a healthy, feisty dog, how could she? After all, they look like a cross

124

between cats and rodents and they were always trespassing in the backyard. Molly had little trouble chasing away the skunks, but she could never quite get out of the way of their spray. It made her eyes burn and water, and when it got in her mouth, it made her choke and gag.

Even worse than the smell or the taste of the skunks were the baths. After her numerous run-ins with skunks, Molly had the following poured on her in an effort to remove their horrible smell - tomato juice, garlic juice, spaghetti sauce, dishwashing liquid, vanilla extract, vinegar and mouthwash. The worst of all was Susan's perfume; it stunk worse than any dog Groomer's shampoo and it made Molly feel like barfing.

The perfume really was the last straw, and Molly never again tangled with a skunk. But now that they were working with the cats... well, she'd just have to risk another perfume bath.

Sasquatch told Molly what he knew about the "situation," which really wasn't very much. All he could report was that the cats were leading a bunch of raccoons and skunks... somewhere.

"But where?" asked Molly.

None of the S.P.O.T.S team could guess where the cats from F.U.S.S. and their allies were heading. Duffy tried to find out, but even with his super vision, he couldn't find any trace of them. Normally this wouldn't have mattered, because like all dogs, Terriers have a very strong sense of smell. It has been said that if there was a single chicken nugget in a fridge three houses away, and that house was on fire, a dog would STILL be able to smell the nugget.

However this time when they sniffed deeply, they caught a faint, distant aroma of skunk, and the stench of the burned quiche that was supposed to be dinner at the house two doors away. But they didn't smell cat.

Just then, they all sensed the same thing at exactly the same moment. Other than food, nothing excites a Terrier as much as a squirrel does. And at that moment, an injured squirrel was limping along a nearby power line. He was desperately trying to get home before the dogs noticed him, but he didn't make it. It only took a faint whiff of squirrel to get the five Terriers barking like crazy.

"SHUT UP!" squawked Sasquatch.

It was a measure of the respect that the Cardinal had gained that Molly, Buck and Duffy actually listened. Georgie was too stubborn to let a bird tell her what to do and Jackie, well, once he got started, he was really hard to stop.

"That squirrel could help us," chirped Sasquatch.

The very idea that a squirrel could, or would, help Terriers was so ridiculous that Duffy and Buck began to laugh. As they giggled, Molly thought carefully. She then nodded and told the other dogs to be quiet.

"Sasquatch is right," said Molly. "The squirrel might know something."

This was a very strange thing for any dog, especially a Terrier, to say. It was such a weird comment that Georgie and Jackie stopped barking and Buck and Duffy's laughter ceased.

Molly looked at the shocked faces of her friends and spoke. "Think about it: the raccoons and skunks are working with the cats. But why aren't the squirrels?"

"Because," said the Cardinal, "cats hate squirrels."

"And the feeling is mutual!" spat out the Squirrel on the wire.

Ten Terrier eyes looked up and beheld a grotesque sight. Something awful had happened to the Squirrel, and most of his fur had been singed away. His tail looked like it belonged to a rat. His right eye was bruised and his left ear had only just begun to scab over.

"Did the cats do that to you?" asked Molly.

"No! HE did it!" yelled the Squirrel as he angrily pointed at Buck.

Buck smiled.

"You'd think I'd remember something that funny."

This made the Squirrel really mad. "How DARE you joke! Remember the nests you blew up? One of them was my home! It took me days to build it!"

With that, the Squirrel ran off down the wire. Sasquatch flew up and landed in front of him.

"Back off bird! This has nothing to do with you!" yelled the Squirrel.

"Yes it does," answered Sasquatch. "The cats are trying to take over the neighborhood, and we're going to stop them."

"Not my problem," answered the Squirrel.

"But we're the good guys!" Barked Molly from twenty feet below the Squirrel.

"Really?! Well, my tail and I don't think you mutts are any good at all!" shrieked the Squirrel.

"Mutts?! Mutts?! MUTTS?!" Yapped Jackie as Georgie, Buck and Duffy began to growl. "We are NOT mutts!"

Molly looked at her angry friends. She understood that they would have been quite happy to either vaporize the rodent or cause it to explode in a thousand stringy, fur-covered pieces. No squirrel had ever insulted Terriers like this. It went against the whole natural order of the neighborhood. But as much as she also wanted to teach the Squirrel a final lesson, Molly knew that they had to be nice in order to discover what the rodent knew.

"Cool it!" she barked at her friends before whispering "we need to find out where the cats are."

The others stopped growling. But their lips twitched and their claws dug into the ground.

"If it calls me a 'mutt' again," threatened Duffy, "it will be the last thing it ever says!"

Realizing that the Terriers could never have a polite conversation with a squirrel, Molly asked Sasquatch to find out what it knew about the cats.

Sasquatch and the Squirrel spoke for a couple of minutes before the Cardinal fluttered down to the dogs with a proposal:

"The squirrel will tell us what he knows if Buck apologizes for destroying his nest."

Buck was unmoved and said, "The day I apologize to a squirrel is the day I pee in a litter box."

"But he knows something about what the cats are doing," protested Sasquatch.

Molly nodded and told Buck that for the good of the neighborhood, he had to apologize.

Buck gritted his teeth as he thought about things. On the one hand was the humiliation of having to be nice to a low-life, bottom of the barrel, garbage-eating, germ-infested, mindless rodent like a squirrel. On the other hand was the humiliation of having the smug, fussy, arrogant, foul-smelling felines strutting around like they ran the neighborhood.

It was a terrible dilemma. One that every dog would dread. Buck looked up at the scarred and sneering squirrel and decided that there was no way he'd ever even speak to such a misbegotten animal.

His decision was final until he looked at his friends who seemed to have made up their minds against him.

"I can't believe you guys think I should say 'sorry' to that fluffy rat."

"What's worse," asked Molly, "one squirrel or five cats?"

"Don't forget," added Georgie "they're working with skunks."

"Raccoons too! Raccoons too!! RACCOONS TOO!!!" yapped Jackie.

"So it's worse than you think," said Duffy, "it's actually one squirrel or five cats, a bunch of skunks and..."

"I get the point!" barked Buck who then turned to Sasquatch. "Tell that rodent that I'm sorry."

"Not good enough," said Sasquatch. "You've got to tell him yourself."

Buck realized that he didn't have much of a choice. He could keep his pride, but that would mean that he and the other members of S.P.O.T.S. would still not know where the cats had headed. Or he could say he was sorry and the team could get on with the mission. Buck sighed heavily and managed to mumble an apology to the Squirrel.

This was a real tribute to Buck. Originally the only regret he had at blowing up the squirrels' homes was that they weren't filled with hundreds and hundreds of the four-legged pests. Just a few hours later, he was being asked to apologize to one of the very rodents that he had tried to eliminate. And he managed to brush his pride aside and humble himself in front of a squirrel.

Good for Buck. What a good boy.

NOT SO FAST

"There's one more thing," said Sasquatch. "He wants ALL of you to promise not to destroy his home, bark at him or chase him out of your families' garbage."

The Terriers' lips curled in disgust and their eyes widened in anger.

Buck had to smile at his friends' discomfort. They now understood how bad it felt for him to have to be nice to a squirrel. He couldn't resist rubbing it in.

"What's worse," he asked, "one squirrel? Or five cats, a bunch of raccoons and some skunks?"

If he wasn't so frantic, Sasquatch would have laughed.

"Dogs!" he chirped once again while shaking his tufted head. "Just say that you agree so we can get a move on."

Molly let out a deep sigh and tilted her head up to face the Squirrel.

"Okay squirrel, here's the deal..." but Molly was interrupted by the Squirrel.

"No deals! You want the info, you do what I ask!"

"DON'T PUSH IT RODENT!" snarled Molly.

The Squirrel froze in terror, and the other Terriers stepped back in surprise. This was a side of Molly that they hadn't seen since the Mailman tried to say "hello" to Emma.

"Here's how things are going to be: we won't destroy your house or chase you. But if we see you in our families' garbage, you'll be in BIG trouble. Got it?!"

The Squirrel nodded. He understood that Molly had just concluded the negotiations.

"Now," panted Molly who always got tired after she had to growl loudly. "What did you see?"

The Squirrel was worried that another squirrel might see him ratting out the cats, so he walked about half way down the lamp post. Low enough to be able to tell the Terriers what he knew, but high enough that none of them could jump up and sink their teeth into him.

"You didn't hear it from me..." the Squirrel began, "but the cats were on their way to the grocery store. Rumor has it that they are going to rob the place."

The grocery store! The best smelling place in the neighborhood. To the Terriers, it was as mysterious and wonderful as a long-hidden Pharaoh's tomb. None of the neighborhood dogs had ever been inside, but they had all shared stories about what they thought was inside.

"Meat!"

"Cheese!"

"Dog snacks!"

"Meat!"

"Bread!"

"Cookies!"

"Peanut Butter!"

"Meat!"

And now the Terriers were going to the store. Better yet, they were going in. They didn't have a choice: the fate of the entire neighborhood was at stake!

"Ummm, can I come with you guys?" asked the Squirrel.

"No!" Molly, Buck, Georgie and Duffy answered.

"No! No! NO!" added Jackie.

"Then could you bring me back a bag of peanuts?"

Molly snarled and turned her back. She had wasted enough time talking to the squirrel. It was time for action.

"Okay. This is it! S.P.O.T.S.! Let's go!"

A STINKY SITUATION

The Terriers were angry and excited as they rushed off. They were angry that the cats would dare to invade the store. And they were excited that they would soon be entering the gates of paradise. They would have been running at full speed, but because of Molly, they only half-ran as Sasquatch flew above them chirping out tweets of encouragement. But they trotted with a real sense of purpose. A feeling of determination. And a burning desire to see what the inside of a grocery store looked like.

As they got closer to the store, their noses were attacked by an absolutely horrifying mix of smells. The shocking scent of skunks mingled with the raunchy reek of raccoons and a fleeting funk of feline fragrance. The resulting stink was so strong that it completely overpowered the glorious, golden aroma of the grocery store.

When they reached the empty parking lot at the back of the store, Molly signaled for the others to stop.

"We can't just run in there," she panted. "The cats may have set a trap."

Molly turned to Duffy and asked if he could see anything inside the store.

Duffy concentrated and used his super vision to see through the wall.

"I saw a couple of them moving near the back."

"If that's where they are," said Molly, "then that's how we'll get into the store."

"I get it! I get it!! I GET IT!!!" Jackie squealed as he bounced. "We'll surprise them and..."

Buck slapped a paw over Jackie's mouth and signaled for him to be quiet.

"Won't be a surprise if you keep shouting."

"Sorry. Sorry, Sorry." Whispered Jackie.

Molly motioned for the Terriers to follow her as she walked along the dark edge of the parking lot towards the rear of the store. The Terriers tried to walk as quietly as cats. They were quieter than usual, but unlike cats, dogs just <u>have</u> to sniff as they walk. They may have been hard to see, but if you listened carefully, you could hear a steady "sniff" "sniff" "sniff" from the perimeter of the parking lot.

Sasquatch realized that even a half-deaf cat could hear them.

"They may have super powers," he thought, "but these guys are the worst at sneaking up on things."

He once again muttered "Dogs..." and flew ahead to see if the coast was clear.

The coast was in fact, far from clear. Hiding behind a fence along the side of the parking lot was a gang of eight skunks.

Now, this wasn't just any group of skunks. The cats had enlisted the help of the most bizarre gang of skunks in the city. They were called the "Mamiferoes do Fedor" which is Portuguese for "mammals of the stench." In a less literal translation it means "smelly mammals." In English, it's an insult, but if you say it in Portuguese, it almost sounds classy.

The leader of the skunks - Vascodor de Gama - named the gang in honor of his great, great, great grandfather who used to raid the garbage bins behind the Portuguese Embassy. None of Vascodor's family had ever been to Portugal, but the stories of the elder skunk's exploits behind the Embassy had been passed down from generation to generation. Once, Vascodor's father brought a shredded piece of a takeout menu from a Portuguese restaurant back to the family den. Vascodor practically grew up looking at the menu fragment's pictures of Lisbon and a leg of roast chicken. To him, Portugal represented everything that was classy, respectable and well-cooked in the world.

Which is not to say that Vascodor was either classy or respectable. He was just an average skunk. A tic-infested garbage shredder who loved nothing better than spraying a mist of seven major volatile chemical components at more popular mammals like dogs. So at this very moment, as Molly led the Terriers towards an ambush by his gang of "Mamiferoes," Vascodor was as happy as a skunk can get.

He raised a paw and whispered "pronto... alvo..." which means "ready... aim..." in Portuguese.

That's when Sasquatch saw the line of black tails with white stripes. He tried to cheep out a warning, but before the sound escaped from his beak, Vascodor shot a load of skunk spray at him. Vascodor's aim was true, and Sasquatch was coated from head to talon. The spray left him temporarily blinded and disoriented, and he sailed over the store like a bird-shaped stink bomb.

The dogs may not have seen Sasquatch shoot past, but they sure could smell Vascodor's stench.

"Retreat!" yelled Molly just as Vascodor gave the command to "FOGO!"

Eight skunks (or, in Portuguese "oito jaritataca") unleashed a cloud of noxious, burning spray. It moved fast, and the Terriers went down hard as the skunks' mist attacked their sinuses and burned their eyes.

Georgie struggled to catch her breath before turning towards the skunks to unleash a super bark. Unfortunately, the skunk spray had inflamed her throat, making it impossible for her to bark. All that came out of Georgie's mouth was a quiet gurgle.

As the Terriers backed away from the skunks, Vascodor snarled in his fake Portuguese accent. "Come back and take your next dose of us!"

Like the others, Jackie's eyes were burning and his vision was obscured. But no amount of pain was going to stop him from getting at the skunks. So Jackie sped towards where he thought the skunks were hiding. He ran with speed, commitment and blind anger. Which meant that he was running as fast as he could when he smashed into the fence.

Jackie was only slightly hurt and had little trouble chewing through the fence. He did however have trouble finding the skunks. Due to the burning in his eyes, he couldn't keep them open for more than a half-second at a time.

"Where, where, WHERE ARE THEY?!" screeched Jackie.

"I don't know!" barked back Duffy who was desperately wiping his eyes on a small patch of grass next to the parking lot. "But when I find them, they are going to be unbelievably sorry!"

"Aqui eu estou!" (or "here I am!") sneered Vascodor. "E eu nao sou ainda pesaroso!" ("And I am not sorry yet!").

He then shot another load of spray at Jackie.

"I'm hit! I'm hit!! I'M HIT!!!" shrieked Jackie.

The sound of Jackie in pain was too much for Molly. She struggled to her feet and took a number of deep breaths.

"I'm coming Jackie!" she growled before taking off at full speed...

...in the opposite direction of the skunks. The blinded Terriers listened intently in order to hear Molly plow into the skunks and teach them a lesson about messing with dogs.

And they listened. And listened. And listened...

Finally, they heard a smash and a crash as Molly ran into a lamp post that fell onto the road.

Molly was howling in pain as she staggered back towards the others.

Buck was fed up. Even though he had taken a big load of spray in his mouth and face, it was time for him to punish the skunks. His throat was raw, his eyes burned and his mouth was throbbing, but he stalked forward like a predator about to crush its prey. The skunks watched in fear as Buck bared his teeth and snarled. Vascodor felt a chill run down his spine. He turned to his Mamiferoes de Fedor and gave the order:

"Tiro neles outra vez!"

But the skunks couldn't "shoot again." They were out of spray, and they realized that Buck wasn't going to wait around for their scent glands to refill. So Vascodor and his gang decided to scare away Buck with their other defense mechanism. This turned out to be a lot less effective than their noxious spray. Even if Buck wasn't so angry, it's doubtful that the sight of a line of skunks stamping their feet would have scared him in the least.

When he was within a few feet of the rodents, Buck inhaled deeply and prepared to unleash a blast of super breath. Buck winced in pain, as his throat still burned from the skunk spray. The pain only made him angrier.

"What are you doing cao?" Vascodor's voice was more pleading than questioning.

"It's called getting even," drawled Buck.

The skunks were now stamping their feet faster and faster in a desperate attempt to scare Buck. It didn't work, and he unleashed what could be called a "super breath." Except that what flowed out of his burning, irritated throat wasn't a breath at all. It was a brown, lava-like flood that instantly incinerated the skunks.

A moment later, Sasquatch fluttered over and was amazed to see that all that remained of their recently formidable enemies was a large puddle of skunk DNA. That, and the horrible odor that clung to the Terriers.

But as bad as they smelled, they had managed to defeat a well-organized and truly dangerous opponent. Sasquatch smiled as he realized that he was part of a formidable team.

DUMPSTER OF DOOM

With the skunks taken care of, the five stinking Super Terriers and the aromatic Cardinal marched and flew towards the rear doors of the grocery store.

A crashing noise from one of the huge garbage dumpsters stopped them in their tracks. Duffy used his super vision, and saw three raccoons in the dumpster foraging through the grocery store's trash. Nothing unusual about that, except that the raccoons were piling up the garbage instead of eating it.

"I see three raccoons in there. It's another ambush!" warned Duffy.

The Terriers assumed attack positions as they faced the dumpster.

"Hold on!" cheeped Sasquatch. "The owl told me the cats were traveling with eight raccoons."

"So where, where, WHERE are the others?" asked Jackie.

"We'll get them later," said Buck. "Let's deal with these ones first."

"We know you're in there!" Molly barked at the dumpster. "Give up now if you know what's good for you."

A pair of black rimmed eyes rose above the rim of the dumpster.

"We will never surrender," squeaked a nervous voice.

"I know that raccoon," growled Georgie. "I chased him out of my backyard last week."

"And now... now it's time for payback!" the Raccoon taunted as his two partners rose from the trash.

Before the Terriers could hurl a snappy comeback at them, the raccoons began to throw mushy brown bananas, green loaves of bread and calcified salami chubs. Raccoons' paws are kind of small, so they had trouble throwing their weapons, and the hailstorm of rotting food was easy for the Terriers to avoid.

"Lets get, get GET them!" snarled Jackie as bottles of expired sunscreen exploded all around him.

As has been mentioned before, Molly was usually a calm, levelheaded Bull Terrier. But something about being pelted with garbage by raccoons changed her. Molly ducked a package of broken linguine sticks and began to growl. None of the other Terriers had ever seen her quite this angry.

"I will not take this from a raccoon!"

Molly's rage turned to action as one of the raccoons in the dumpster threw a dented tin of sardines. Molly snarled and ran faster than a Saluki towards the dumpster.

The other Terriers looked away as Molly slammed into the dumpster at full speed. There was a tremendous BAM!!!

and three raccoons screeched in unison (and in fear) (AND in raccoon language) as the garbage-filled dumpster rose into the air.

Considering that it was a dumpster, it looked fairly graceful as it reached its apex high above the vacant lot behind the grocery store. As it began its descent though, it quickly stopped looking graceful. That's when the dumpster spun over and dropped bags of garbage and rotting vegetables.

Inside the dumpster, the three raccoons had to make a quick decision. Unfortunately for them, they had trouble choosing a plan of action.

The First Raccoon grunted that they had a better chance of survival if they dove clear of the dumpster. The Second One yelled that the First Raccoon was a "flea-filled fool" and that the layers of trash would help to cushion the impact. The Third Raccoon could see the point of each of the arguments. But somehow, he thought there had to be a third way to do things. Maybe if they checked the dumpster for empty juice boxes, they could build themselves crash-protective suits that would...

The dumpster slamming into the ground made it hard for him to finish his thought. The impact was so strong that it formed a crater in the soft ground of the vacant lot.

The noise of the crashing dumpster echoed through the neighborhood for a moment. Then, all was silent except for the sound of Molly's angry panting.

Buck, Georgie, Duffy and Jackie walked over to their leader. Sasquatch fluttered overhead. Without a word, the six heroes-to-be walked and flew past the crashed dumpster and towards the rear entrance of the store.

At last the time had come for them to confront the cats.

INTO THE STORE

It was up to Georgie to get them into the store. She took a deep breath and unleashed a loud, sharp bark that sent the door flying off its hinges and far into the store.

"Be careful," said Molly. "Cats are a lot smarter than raccoons."

"But they aren't as smart as Terriers!" shouted Georgie.

With that, the S.P.O.T.S. rushed into the darkened building that they had so often dreamed about. The five of them took a deep breath, as they were sure that the wonderful food smells of the store would be stronger than the putrid skunk aroma that seemed to be stuck to them.

But as they inhaled, the smell receptors in their brains registered the scent of the liquid laundry detergent that covered the floor. Before they could figure out the significance of this smell, the Terriers were sliding across the slick, soapy floor towards the frozen food section. When they hit the freezer cases at full speed, the Terriers yelped in surprise and outrage. None of them imagined that their entry into the holiest shrine in the dog world would be quite so painful.

"The cats did this!" growled Duffy, proving for the first time in a number of chapters that he had a gift for stating that which is REALLY obvious.

As the Terriers struggled to their feet they heard a familiar and unwelcome voice.

"Tho, you made it patht our thentrieth." It was Peter. And he was close. Real close.

"Hey cat, cat, CAT!" yelled Jackie. "What are 'thentrieth'?"

Peter hissed angrily. It was up to Molly to clarify that Peter meant to say "sentries." Which is a fancy way of saying "guards."

Jackie was still confused. All he'd seen were skunks and raccoons. As Molly patiently explained that the skunks and raccoons were the guards, or "thentrieth," a bottle of olive oil crashed on the floor in front of them. The floor was even more slippery and was now also covered with broken glass.

"We can't walk on glass," said Duffy. Which again, wasn't exactly breaking news.

Another bottle exploded nearby. The Terriers would have been trapped if Molly didn't have an idea.

"Sasquatch..." she whispered to the bird. "The cats can see in the dark, but we can't. We need to even things up."

Sasquatch smiled and nodded as he flew off to find the light switch.

From atop the Italian food shelves, Peter hissed down at the dogs.

"Admit it: You sthmelly, sthuper sthtupid Terrierth are no match for uth".

After a lengthy and uncomfortable silence, Peter finally realized that none of the Terriers would ever admit such a thing. Unable to think of any further taunts, Peter threw one more bottle of oil before running off to supervise the looting of the store.

Meanwhile, Sasquatch was flying in the dark, desperately trying to find the light switch without being noticed by the cats. Unfortunately for him, Cardinals, like dogs, have trouble seeing in the dark. After flying into a hanging sign that promised "Lowest Prices EVER!!" Sasquatch let out a "cheep" of frustration.

Come to think of it, he may have been commenting on the sign's slogan by saying that the store's prices were "cheap."

In any event, he was lucky that either the "cheep" or the "cheap" wasn't noticed by the cats. Luckier still was the fact that it was heard by a family of starlings that lived on a beam near the ceiling.

Daddy Starling quietly called out to Sasquatch; "Who's there?"

Sasquatch fluttered over to their nest and introduced himself. He then told the birds that he was trying to help a bunch of dogs get the cats out of the store.

Like all birds, Daddy Starling hated cats. So he was more than happy to help. He led Sasquatch to the light switch at the front of the store. The two birds worked together, pecking at the switch in unison until they finally got the lights turned on.

As light filled the store, the two birds beheld an incredible sight. Five raccoons were tied to the front of shopping carts that were being loaded by Patches, Precious, Puss Puss and Petunia. The cats were using their huge, gross tongues to drop boxes, bottles and cans into the carts.

Peter stood with his back arched in front of the raccoons. He was hissing wildly to keep them in line.

"Ligth or no ligth. You sthtay here until I thay tho!"

Sasquatch and Daddy Starling exchanged a shocked look.

"The cats are in control of the store," moaned Daddy Starling. "What kind of a world is this?!"

"I have to tell the team!" chirped Sasquatch.

Before he could take off, a flying hairball whizzed between the two birds' heads.

"You birds are going nowhere!" snarled Patches as he prepared to hoark up another missile.

The birds quickly flew away in opposite directions: Daddy Starling went to protect his family while Sasquatch soared towards the back of the store. He hadn't gone far when one of Patches's hairballs splooshed into him and knocked

S.P.O.T.S.

him off course. The pain was excruciating, but Sasquatch kept on flying.

While that was going on, the Terriers were surveying their surroundings. The broken glass was confined to one small area in front of them and the floor was thick with olive oil. But if they stepped carefully, they could begin their chasing of the cats.

The Terriers looked past the obstacles and into the main part of the store. The view was awe inspiring. There was row after row of human food. Shelves filled with bread, peanut butter, potato chips and thousands of other delicacies. There were also racks filled with dog food, dog treats, dog cookies, squeaky toys, pig ears and imitation pig ears for dogs with humans who were vegetarians. Oddly, the shelves next to the dog food were empty. It was Buck who figured out why.

"They're stealing the cat food," he murmured.

Other racks were decimated as well. The extent of the cat's thievery was truly shocking. The canned salmon and tuna were gone. It didn't look like there was a single package of cold cuts left in the store. And the dairy section looked like it had been hit by a tornado.

"Those lowlifes have no respect," growled Duffy. "They're destroying the store!"

As Molly led the Terriers through the oil and around the broken glass, she wondered how five cats could have stolen so much food. She was trying to figure things out when she saw something beautiful. Molly stopped and gazed in wonder. The others also noticed...

A MEATY TRAP

Steaks.

Five thick juicy steaks.

Just sitting there. Glistening in the light. Waiting for dog teeth to sink into them.

Steak...

"Steak... Steak..." the five Terriers repeated as they stepped forward in a zombie-like trance.

"Steak ... Steak ... STEAK!!!..."

The smell of the meat overwhelmed their senses. Grunts and whines of anticipation filled the air as they stepped up to the beef.

"Seems too good to be true," said Buck.

S.P.O.T.S.

"Do they always have meat on the floor?" wondered Georgie.

"This really is the best, best BEST place in the world!" said Jackie. The others nodded.

Even a hungry dog realizes that a steak is a rare treat, and so it should be savored. That's why the Terriers didn't simply attack the steaks. Instead, they sniffed them carefully and lovingly.

Which was a good thing. Because as they were sniffing, Molly caught a whiff of something unpleasant. Not as bad as the skunk smell that clung to them: this was more like a fake flower smell. The kind of smell that she recognized from the times when Susan cleaned the washroom.

"STOP!" she barked. "It's a trap!"

Molly picked up her steak and flipped it over. Sure enough, the bottom of the meat was covered in a white paste.

It sure looked like the stuff that Susan used when she was cleaning the house. Since Susan wore rubber gloves when she used the paste, Molly figured that it was not something that the Terriers should be eating.

"The cats have covered the meat with poison!" she barked.

"Knew it was too good to be true," Buck said sadly as he and the others backed away from the meat.

"Guys! Guys!" cheeped Sasquatch as he swooped down to join the Terriers. When he landed, a chunk of a hairball fell off of his wing and landed on a steak.

"You've been hit!" Duffy said unnecessarily.

After Sasquatch assured the Terriers that he was okay, Molly told him about the steaks. Sasquatch shook his head. Truly, the cats' capacity for evil was limitless.

He then reported that the Owl had been right - the cats did have eight raccoons working with them. Three of them were flattened like furry pancakes in the upside down dumpster. The other five were pulling shopping carts filled with food and cat treats out of the store.

"They've stolen a lot of stuff," said Sasquatch.

"And we're going to thteal a lot more!" Peter snarled from the top of the breakfast food aisle as he threw a bottle of maple syrup at the Terriers.

After diving out of the way of the shattering syrup bottle, the Terriers were pelted by high-calibre hairballs that seemed to come from every direction.

The Terriers looked around and saw that the cats were standing in different aisles. Peter was with the cereals and pancake mixes while Petunia was flexing his super-size claws in the "Foods of the World" section. Precious snarled from amidst the medicines and toiletries. In the snack food aisle, Patches was snapping his tongue like a pink whip. Over in the dairy row, Puss Puss slashed open a bag of milk. The white liquid shot up like a gushing oil well, and Puss Puss opened wide and caught some of it in his mouth.

The sight of this vandalism in such a holy site made the Terriers growl.

"You can't do that," snarled Buck.

"Wrong Bucko!" purred Puss Puss. "I just DID do that!"

Molly had seen enough. She put out her paw and barked "Time for the Super Powerful Organization of Terriers..."

"...and Songbird," added Sasquatch as he put his wing tip on top of Molly's paw.

Buck, Duffy, Georgie and Jackie added their paws to the pile as Molly continued...

"...to take back this store!"

And with that, the Terrific Terriers turned to face the far less terrific cats.

"Let's do this!" snarled Molly.

"Let'th do thith!" hissed back Peter.

THE FINAL SHOWDOWN

It was time for the big fight. Time to see which of the world's two most popular types of house pets would run the neighborhood. Each of the Terriers chose a cat to fight and then ran off to do battle.

The shortest fight started when Georgie ran into the "Foods of the World" aisle to face Petunia. In case you've forgotten about Petunia, he was very large for a cat, very fluffy for a cat and not very bright for a cat. Petunia thought that he could intimidate Georgie just by slowly waving his claws in front of her.

"Scared?" he asked before answering the question himself. "Well, you should be."

"I'm a Westie you goof ball," Georgie sneered in response. "We fear no cat."

To prove her point, Georgie let out a deep, glass-shattering bark. Which was a really good strategy, as the shelves on either side of Petunia were stacked with glass bottles filled with foods from all over the world.

The bark caused the bottles to explode. Petunia was quickly covered in chutney, tahini, refried beans and dulce de leche. The combination of sticky mango jam, thick sesame seed paste, gooey, spicy bean puree and sweet caramel sauce created a goo that was more adhesive than the craziest of glues. And that goo was all over Petunia.

Georgie let out a second bark and Petunia instinctively covered his ears with his paws. Sadly for him, his paws were so syrupy that they stuck to the hairs on his ears. Georgie was kind of disappointed that Petunia didn't put up more of a fight. She did however like the sight of the paste and jam covered cat struggling to pull his paws off of his ears.

While Georgie was turning Petunia into a helpless, sticky mess, Jackie and Precious were having a high-speed chase up and down the pharmaceutical and toiletry aisle. Precious used his claws to grab onto diaper packages in order to climb out of range of Jackie's snapping super jaws. When he got to the top of the shelf, Precious spat super-powered hairballs that barely missed their mark.

"You, you, YOU!" spluttered the enraged Jackie, "are going down!"

Jackie attacked the shelves and began to chomp his way through them. The taste of shredded diapers and shampoo were hard to deal with, but after the nightmare of the skunk spray, he could handle it.

"Well dog," said Precious, "for once you're right. I _am_ going down."

Precious stood like a high diver and jumped, long claws out, towards Jackie. Luckily, Jackie saw a glint of claw and rolled out of the way at the very last second. Even so, one of Precious' claws clipped Jackie on his hip. It left a shallow cut, but one of the things that Jack Russells do better than almost any other breed is overreact.

Jackie let out a shriek that would have been blood curdling... if blood could actually curdle. He was too angry to remember Molly warning the Terriers to be careful because cats were pretty smart. If Jackie had remembered this, he might have thought twice before he chased after Precious when the cat ran up the aisle.

The pharmacy sections of many grocery stores have special chairs that old people sit in when they want to measure their blood pressure. They consist of a padded seat on a metal frame with a tube for people's arms. Inside the tube is a rubber cuff that inflates to squeeze the upper arm. Somehow, this contraption gauges a person's blood pressure.

Precious squeezed himself through the arm tube, and when he emerged, he smacked the red "start" button. If Jackie weren't so angry, or hyper, he would have tried to figure out why Precious pushed the button. But he <u>was</u> angry, and he <u>was</u> hyper, so he couldn't stop himself. Which is why he tried to squeeze through the narrow tube just as the rubber blood pressure cuff began to inflate.

Jackie was stuck. It was embarrassing, painful, frustrating and extremely dangerous. Slowly but surely, the cuff inflated. Jackie went from being unable to escape to being unable to breathe. In just a few seconds, the cuff would crush him.

"I can't believe you fell for that," taunted Precious. "I guess it's true what I say: I'm more than just another pretty, kitty face."

Jackie's eyes bulged and what was starting to seem like his final breath was being squeezed out of him. Needless to say, he couldn't come up with an insult for Precious.

"Why so quiet mutt; cat got your tongue?"

Precious cackled at his terrible joke. He was still laughing as Jackie bent his neck so he could get his teeth on the edge of the cuff. When his mouth was over the tube, he summoned the last dregs of his strength and bit down.

The imprisoning tube cracked as Jackie's teeth bit through the metal. The cuff quickly deflated as it was pierced by his canines. Small Terriers tend to revive quickly, so it only took a single breath for Jackie to get back to full strength. Which meant that his teeth and jaws were back to super strength. Which meant that Precious was still snickering as Jackie scurried out of the arm tube and picked the entire chair up in his mouth. The cat's brain had just started to send the signal to run when the large metal chair came crashing down on top of him.

Jackie took a couple more deep breaths before walking over to the fallen cat. Precious was stunned but was otherwise fine. If "fine" can mean being trapped under a four hundred pound chair. There was a horrible screeching sound as Precious' super claws desperately tried to rip through the thick metal of the chair. Jackie smiled, as he knew it would take Precious hours to scratch out a cat-sized hole.

Precious hissed weakly. "This isn't over dog."

"It sure, sure, SURE looks like it is!" gloated Jackie.

Over in the dairy section, Puss Puss laughed in Duffy's snarling face.

"Real scary," said the cat sarcastically. "You look like a stuffed toy."

"Shut up cat!" snapped Duffy who actually did look more like a stuffed toy than a real dog.

"Forget what I said," snarled Puss Puss. "Your smell is too putrid for you to be a stuffed toy."

Duffy bared his teeth and sprinted towards Puss Puss who held his ground. In a situation like this, a Dandy Dinmont usually wishes that he or she was bigger and more intimidating. As a breed, they are keenly aware that they don't frighten anyone other than squirrels.

In addition to wishing that he was scarier looking, Duffy now wished that he had a power other than super vision. Sure, he could see Puss Puss clearly enough, but he would have been much happier to be able to unleash a gust of super breath or a loud head-shattering bark. No such luck for Duffy who didn't even need his super vision to see Puss Puss shoot out his unbelievably long tongue.

He tried to swerve out of the way, but the tongue whipped, caught him and flicked him up and into the nearly empty milk fridge. Duffy would have been badly hurt if it wasn't for the row of untouched buttermilk jugs that he crashed into. The jugs split open and coated Duffy with what has to be the most disgusting and smelly product made from anything to do with cows.

Humiliated and soaked with the raunchy, lactosey badness of buttermilk, Duffy wondered how he was going to defeat the cat. Crouching as low as he could, he crawled along inside the milk fridge. He used his super vision to watch Puss Puss who was busy licking his paws so he could clean and groom himself.

"Who cleans themselves during a fight?" wondered Duffy.

The obvious answer was "cats." They are so obsessed with cleanliness that it's a wonder they don't use alcohol wipes to clean their paws.

As Puss Puss began to lick his hip, Duffy had an idea. Being coated in buttermilk, dirt and skunk smell gave him a weapon that Puss Puss would fear; the weapon of grossness. Once he jumped on the cat and spread some of his buttermilky filth, Duffy would be battling a severely freaked-out opponent.

All that Duffy needed was a chance to sneak up on Puss Puss. And to do that, he needed a diversion.

It seemed as though Sasquatch was either reading Duffy's mind, or this page, because at that very moment, he flew down the aisle and swooped threateningly at Puss Puss. The shocked cat turned and swiped his long claws at Sasquatch. He missed, and Duffy seized the opportunity to leap out of the milk fridge. A dog with longer legs would have been on Puss Puss in a single bound. Duffy made it in two and a half bounds.

As he landed on Puss Puss's back, Duffy performed a very strange move for a dog in a fight. He didn't bite or scratch. Instead, he hugged and squeezed. Puss Puss shook as if he'd been electrocuted. The stench from the Terrier was horrifying. Puss Puss' eyes watered as if he was having an allergic reaction to the skunky buttermilk stench. Even worse than the smell was the feeling of having chunky milk and dirt smeared onto his skin.

Puss Puss let out a long, shocked howl and squirmed like a crazy cat. This made things worse as rubbing against Duffy activated his super static power. Duffy clung even tighter.

The smell was making Puss Puss lightheaded. He quickly did an inventory of his super powers to see if he could get rid of the dog before he passed out. The projectile hairballs couldn't be deployed as Duffy's head was directly behind his own and the shots were sure to miss. The static power was partially responsible for his current predicament, and the thought of using his tongue made him gag. Tasting Duffy's skunky fur when he flung him into the dairy case was bad enough. No way was he going to wrap his tongue around him to try to yank him off. That would take about ten seconds of tasting dog, skunk, dirt and buttermilk. Which was about eleven seconds too many.

Slowly, a smile formed on Puss Puss' face. Why panic when he had very long and very sharp claws? With just a couple of swings, Puss Puss could hurt Duffy so badly that the dog wouldn't be able to stand up again, let alone inflict his stench on him.

Puss Puss relaxed and held up his front paws. The claws slowly slid out and glinted menacingly in the light.

"Just look at what I brought," he sneered. "This is going to REALLY hurt."

"Duffy, let go!" Sasquatch called as he swooped down at Puss Puss.

The cat momentarily forgot about the smelly Terrier and instead swung his claws at Sasquatch. Duffy saw the claws and tore himself off of Puss Puss.

As Duffy backed away, he tried to figure out his next move. Before he could come up with a single useful idea as to how to defeat a violent and heavily armed opponent, he heard the flapping of many sets of wings. He looked up and saw Sasquatch along with an entire family of starlings as they landed on the light fixtures above the aisle. Each bird occupied a different fixture, and as Duffy made eye contact with Sasquatch, the Cardinal winked mischievously.

Still unsure of what to do, Duffy continued to back away from Puss Puss who waved his claws menacingly.

"Okay Terrier, this is it! I've had more than enough of you!"

To Duffy's amazement and horror, Puss Puss' claws grew even longer as he prepared to pounce. He closed his eyes in fear as Puss Puss reared up on his hind legs, howled and prepared to pounce. Duffy didn't see what happened next, but he did hear it. It sounded like this...

"Plop."

Duffy opened his eyes and saw Puss Puss' gaping mouth as it formed a silent scream. The cat was so upset that he couldn't even make a sound. What was upsetting him was a splat of Cardinal dropping that had landed on his head.

Luckily for him, Puss Puss remembered to retract his claws before trying to wipe the mess of his head.

"Plop."

Sasquatch's aim was perfect. Puss Puss looked at the bird mess on his hand and finally found his voice.

"NOOOOO!!!!"

Cats hate being messy. And there are just no words that can properly describe how they feel when they get <u>this</u> type of messy. It got worse, because as Puss Puss jumped around in panic, the Starling family let fly. More accurately, they let drop. Not all of their efforts hit Puss Puss, but enough of them hit the feline target to send him halfway to Breakdown City.

Which is located close to both Mental Cat Corners and Crazy Kitty Village.

When Duffy last saw Puss Puss, he was running out of the store in a complete frenzy trying to figure out how he was going to clean himself.

Duffy looked up at Sasquatch and the Starling family and barked a happy "thanks guys." Never again would he doubt that Sasquatch was a valuable member of the team. From now on, he'd always call their group the "Super Powerful Organization of Terriers and Songbird." As far as Duffy was now concerned, "S.P.O.T.S." really did have a nice ring to it.

Nearby in the beverage section, Buck and Patches faced each other from opposite ends of a long aisle. It was like a duel from an old western movie, except that there were eight combined legs instead of four.

First Patches would take a step forward, and then Buck would do the same.

Patches.

Buck.

Patches.

Buck.

With each step forward, the duelists made a comment. First Patches said "Just you and me Buck." Then Buck said "Just you and me Patches." Then Patches said "you're going to be sorry," which was immediately followed by Buck saying "No, you're going to be sorry." Then came Patches' question of "Any last words?" and Buck answered with a question of his own; "Any last words?" Technically, that wasn't really a question of his own, but his accent made it sound a bit different than when Patches had asked it.

They continued on like this for five more small steps. You don't need all the details of their conversation, because it really became quite boring after a while.

Finally, the two of them stopped stalking forward. Buck looked at Patches and noticed for the first time how big he was. But unlike most big cats, Patches wasn't just a fur-covered blob. He was a muscular beast who looked like he got a lot of exercise. Buck stared at Patches' ugly, scarred face. No doubt about it, Patches must have stayed fit by beating up on other cats. In a word, he looked like a "bully."

Meanwhile, Patches was looking at Buck. The only thought going through his mind was how much fun he was going to have while beating the daylights out of the Irish Terrier. As is the case with many good fighters, Patches liked to visualize his battles. Patches figured he'd start by using his tongue to grab a nearby jumbo bottle of root beer which he would then hurl at Buck. While the Terrier was off balance, Patches would shoot some high-speed hairballs towards his stomach. After they found their target, Buck would be too winded to unleash one of his super breaths. And that's when Patches would pounce with his long claws.

"Yeah," thought Patches, "that's what I'm going to do."

Patches never did get the chance to put his plan in motion. Exactly three seconds after he finished his thought, and two seconds before he would have attacked, a rack of sports drinks fell on him, knocking him out cold.

As all of the dog versus cat battles were happening simultaneously, there's a logical reason as to why a rack of artificially flavored, colored and sweetened "health" drinks fell on top of Patches.

And to find that reason, we have to move to the next aisle and go back precisely four minutes in time. For that was when angry Molly stomped into the breakfast food aisle just in time to see Peter climb to the top of a rack.

"You afraid of me Peter?" she asked.

"Ha!" laughed Peter. "Thinth I got my powerth, I fear no dog!"

"Then come down here and we can settle this."

Molly was aching for a fight. She was also just plain aching. Slamming into dumpsters and lampposts is not particularly good for an older dog's body.

The sounds of the fights between the other Terriers and cats could clearly be heard throughout the store. The two leaders listened carefully to try to figure out which side was winning. It was hard to tell until Georgie's bark rang out. As the sound of exploding bottles and falling glass filled the air, Peter had a feeling that the dogs would soon have the upper hand. That's why he offered Molly a deal...

"The neighborhood ith big enough for dogth AND cath. Leth thplit it in half. You guyth can do whatever you want to the rodenth and other mammalth. Juth leave the birdth to uth."

Molly thought about her new friend Sasquatch. There was no way she'd agree to anything that would put him, or others like him at the mercy of a bunch of powerful and nasty cats.

"No deal Peter. This fight isn't about controlling the neighborhood." Molly said. "It's about keeping it safe for everyone and everything."

"Even thquirrelth and racoonth?" Peter asked.

Molly sighed heavily before nodding.

"Even squirrels and raccoons. Unless they do something that hurts the neighborhood."

"Hmmm," said Peter dramatically. "Would your familyth garden be part of the neighborhood?"

Molly's eyes widened in anger.

"Are you threatening Susan's garden?" she growled.

Peter sneered. "Put it thith way; after they finish hiding our food, the raccoonth are going to vithit the garden. I told them it'th filled with berrieth."

Molly's eyes widened further with anger. If they opened any further, her eye balls would have fallen out.

"You leave the garden alone," she growled.

"Oh, I will," answered Peter. "If you agree to my termth."

Feeling that his extortion had worked, Peter leaned down.

"Tho? Do we have a deal?" he asked.

Sometimes good people and good dogs are confronted with something or someone that is just plain bad. In this case it was a cat that was born mean, grew up spoiled and angry and would live its entire life thinking up nasty things to do. Every single thing that a character like this does is done for its own gain. The feelings of others - even of his team mates - meant nothing to him. There could be no doubt that any deal that Peter offered was not one that would benefit the Terriers or the neighborhood.

For a good dog with super powers there really was only one thing to do. And that thing was to run at full speed into the rack of granola that Peter was sitting on. The force of the collision between Molly and the rack sent Peter shooting through the air. It also caused the rack - which had granola on one side and "sport" and "health" drinks on the other - to fall into the next aisle where it flattened Patches.

Back in that aisle, Buck looked at the fallen rack and the pile of drinks and cereal boxes that covered the prone Patches.

"Well," he drawled, "that was easy."

"Not really," groaned Molly who was now REALLY aching. "You see where Peter ended up?"

Buck shook his head. Within the next minute or so, the other three dog versus cat battles ended. It was a clean sweep for the good guys as they beat the cats 5-0. The only damage seemed to be the scratch on Jackie's hip...

"Not a scratch!" he argued, "it's a deep, deep, DEEP gash!"

...and the absolutely rancid stench coming off of Duffy. But all things considered, it was a good night for the "Super Powerful Organization of Terriers."

"And Songbird," added Duffy as Sasquatch rejoined the team.

Before they could call it "Mission Accomplished" however, there was the matter of the stolen food and Susan's garden. Molly told the others that she was too tired to chase any more bad mammals. Buck, who was disappointed at not getting a chance to do any actual fighting, volunteered to take care of the raccoons. With that, he stepped over the pile of granola and sports drinks and walked slowly towards the door.

"Shouldn't you, like, hurry, hurry HURRY?!" yipped Jackie.

"No need," replied Buck. "With those heavy loads, the raccoons ain't getting too far. Besides, I need to get prepared."

With that, Buck began tasting every food that he saw on the floor of the store. He even lapped at some of the spilled buttermilk. None of the other members of S.P.O.T.S. could be sure what the effect of this diverse and fairly disgusting mix of foods would be on Buck's super breath.

But they could be sure that the next few minutes weren't going to be very pleasant for the raccoons.

AFTER THE BATTLE

After Buck left, the other Terriers walked through the store for one more quick look. None of them knew when, if ever, they'd be back inside.

As they walked up and down the aisles, they saw that Petunia was still stuck to the floor, Precious was safely trapped under the blood pressure chair and Patches was unconscious under a pile of bottles, cans and boxes. They knew that Puss Puss was off somewhere trying desperately to get clean. They couldn't find Peter, but they guessed that he'd gone home to lick his wounds and hide under a couch.

The Terriers were so proud of themselves that they thought about leaving some sort of evidence that they'd been the ones who saved the store. Sasquatch however didn't think the humans who worked at the store would be pleased to find an upside down garbage dumpster, a cat stuck to the floor, another cat trapped under a destroyed blood pressure chair and a third one lying under a small mountain of food and drinks. Add in the rotting, poisoned steaks on the glass-covered floor and the missing food and carts and, well, Sasquatch had a feeling that the Terriers would be smart to be anonymous superheroes for the time being.

Molly and the others took another look around the store and saw that Sasquatch was right. They then rushed out of the store just in case a human was on the way.

Before he flew out, Sasquatch cheeped "goodbye" to the Starlings before pecking off the light.

The Terriers and Sasquatch had just made it across the parking lot when they saw something glowing eerily in the distance. Before Duffy could focus his super vision, Buck moseyed up to them.

"I'm guessing you caught up to the raccoons," said Molly.

Buck smiled.

"I'll just say that adding cheese sticks, gravy, tofu, buttermilk and sauerkraut to my stomach is a bad recipe for raccoons."

"Are they going to be okay?" asked Georgie.

Buck thought for a moment. He then shrugged.

"Does it really matter?"

Sasquatch and the Terriers smiled.

With their first mission a success, and the neighborhood safe, the members of S.P.O.T.S. headed home for a well deserved rest.

Which would unfortunately have to wait until their families stopped yelling at them for running off and smelling like skunks (and buttermilk), and forcing them to take numerous baths. Then, and only then, would they be allowed to get some sleep.

There was also the matter of the unexplainable new holes in the doors of Jackie and Georgie's homes.

But that's something that their families would have to figure out on their own.

After all, there's only so much that a dog can do for its humans.

FRANKLIN YOUNG

Franklin Young works and lives in Toronto where he is the proud husband of one, the proud father of two, and the proud companion to a West Highland Terrier who has mastered the Power of Super Snoring.

Made in the USA
Charleston, SC
13 April 2012